the MYSTERIOUS DISAPPEARANCE of AIDAN S.

(as told to his brother)

ALSO BY DAVID LEVITHAN

Boy Meets Boy

The Realm of Possibility

Are We There Yet?

The Full Spectrum (edited with Billy Merrell)

Marly's Ghost (illustrated by Brian Selznick)

Nick & Norah's Infinite Playlist (written with Rachel Cohn)

Wide Awake

Naomi and Ely's No Kiss List (written with Rachel Cohn)

How They Met, and Other Stories

The Likely Story series (written as David Van Etten, with David Ozanich
and Chris Van Etten)

Love Is the Higher Law

Will Grayson, Will Grayson (written with John Green)

Dash & Lily's Book of Dares (written with Rachel Cohn)

The Lover's Dictionary

Every You, Every Me (with photographs by Jonathan Farmer)

Every Day

Invisibility (written with Andrea Cremer)

Two Boys Kissing

Another Day

Hold Me Closer: The Tiny Cooper Story

You Know Me Well (written with Nina LaCour)

The Twelve Days of Dash & Lily (written with Rachel Cohn)

Sam & Ilsa's Last Hurrah (written with Rachel Cohn)

Someday

Mind the Gap, Dash & Lily (written with Rachel Cohn)

DAVID LEVITHAN

the MYSTERIOUS DISAPPEARANCE of AIDAN S.

(as told to his brother)

Alfred A. Knopf
New York

THIS IS A BORZOI BOOK PUBLISHED BY ALFRED A. KNOPF

Visit us on the Web! rhcbooks.com

Educators and librarians, for a variety of teaching tools, visit us at RHTeachersLibrarians.com

Library of Congress Cataloging-in-Publication Data is available upon request.
ISBN 978-1-9848-4859-8 (trade) — ISBN 978-1-9848-4860-4 (lib. bdg.) —
ISBN 978-1-9848-4861-1 (ebook) — ISBN 978-0-593-37744-4 (intl. tr. pbk.)

The text of this book is set in 11.8-point Gamma ITC Std.
Interior design by Cathy Bobak

Printed in the United States of America
February 2021
10 9 8 7 6 5 4 3 2 1

First Edition

For Ben Lindsay, dear friend

1

They looked everywhere.

The woods behind our backyard. The school. The woods behind the school. The basement. The attic. The pond, even though the pond was a long walk away. They called the parents of every kid in Aidan's class, even the ones who'd moved away.

We opened every door to every room in our house, every door to every closet. We searched every crawl space, checked under every bed. We pulled back each of the shower curtains and looked for footprints in all of the rugs. It was a game of hide and seek that got old after five minutes, alarming after an hour, and the scariest thing that had ever happened to any of us after that.

Aidan couldn't be found.

They asked me the same questions over and over again.

When did you last see him?

I was falling asleep. It was his turn to shut off the lights. I saw him get out of his bed and go to the light switch. Then I heard him get back into bed, and I think we said goodnight.

What time was this?

Around ten?

You're not sure.

That's usually when we turn out the lights. I wasn't paying attention. I just wanted to go to bed.

Were you asleep when he left the room?

I think so. I didn't hear the door.

How long does it take you to go to sleep?

I don't know.

Does your brother usually get up in the middle of the night?

I don't think so.

Have you ever caught him sleepwalking?

No.

Did he say anything to you about running away?

No.

Do you think he ran away?

Only because he's not here. But there's no reason for him to run away. He's twelve.

And you're eleven, Lucas?

Yes.

He didn't say anything unusual to you?

No.

He wasn't mad about anything?

No. And if he was really running away . . .

What?

He would have taken his phone. He wouldn't have left it behind. He loves his games too much.

Is there any place your brother would have gone? Any friends he would have wanted to see?

Late at night? No.

No one.

Glenn's his best friend. But he sees Glenn all the time. I mean, during the day. I don't think they would meet up at night in secret, if that's what you're asking. But I guess you'd have to ask Glenn.

Is there any place your brother goes to hide? Like when you're playing—where does he hide?

The attic. Aidan always hides in the attic.

They checked every inch of the attic. They moved every box, opened every old cupboard, chest, and dresser. There were traces of Aidan up there—footsteps and fingerprints left in the dust. But there were traces of Aidan every-where. This was our house. We lived all over it.

They looked for a note. They looked at the histories of every device Aidan used. They looked in a circle around our house, trying to find a trail. And they also looked for any sign that someone had broken in and stolen him away from us.

So much looking. And they couldn't find a thing.

Did you get into a fight with Aidan?
No.
Did your parents get into a fight with Aidan?
No.
Did you yell at him?
No.
Did they yell at him?
No.
Was there any reason for him to leave?
No.
Are you sure?
Yes.

Neighbors and strangers banded together to search, walking at arm's length through fields and forests, staring at the ground for clues. The pond—they kept coming back to the pond, even though I told them we never went near the pond, because it was on Mr. Magruder's property, and Mr. Magruder had told us to stay away. Even Aidan, who was much braver than I was, or maybe much more reckless than I was, wouldn't go near the pond.

They listened to me, but not really.

An alert was sent out. It was on the news. Reporters asked the people watching to call the number below if they had any information.

Lots of people called, but nobody had any information.

Were the two of you close?
I thought we were. I'm not sure.

We'd always shared a room. For as long as I could remember, sleep meant the two of us breathing the same air, our eyes adjusting to the same darkness. I'd grown used to just about any noise he could make, although there were definitely times I woke up to hear him talking to himself and was surprised by what he was saying. (One time I heard him say "Good job!" and assumed he was complimenting me on my own sleeping.) His snoring could be thunderous—but he said the same thing about my farting.

I knew him. I knew his favorite foods. I knew his least-favorite baseball team. I knew which socks he'd choose to go with which shirt and exactly which grunt he'd make when he felt the game he was playing had cheated him out of a win. We were one year apart, and most of the time people thought I was the older one, even though I wasn't. I paid attention to him, but I didn't pay enough attention to know for sure whether he was paying any attention back.

And, of course, when my attention was needed the most, I failed. I was asleep.

Good job.

Our town wasn't very big, but it seemed much bigger when you were considering all the spaces a twelve-year-old could disappear into. Not just the pond, but the trees. Not just the trees, but the fields. Not just the fields, but the sewers. Not just the sewers, but the houses. Not just the houses, but the stores. The trash cans behind the stores. The cars left unlocked.

Hide and seek.

None of his friends had seen him or talked to him or had any idea where he was. Glenn and his parents came over to our house, but all they could do was feel helpless alongside us. The police asked Glenn if they could talk to him, the same way they'd asked me. As if we had a choice.

Of course we talked to them. Of course we were willing to tell them everything we knew. I assumed they asked Glenn the same questions they asked me, or mostly the same questions. But never at the same time. Whenever Glenn's phone lit up with a text, they asked if it was Aidan. But it was always another friend, wondering what was going on.

I had a phone, but I was only supposed to use it for emergencies. This was an emergency, but the only person I wanted to call about it didn't have his phone.

We kept watch. There was always someone awake. Just in case there was a call. Just in case there was a knock at the door.

We made sure the doors were locked, fearing intruders. You had to knock or ring the doorbell for someone to let you in.

That ended up being important.

Are you sure you can't think of anything else?

One day turned into two days.

Two days turned into three days.

I didn't go to school. Mom and Dad didn't go to work. Mom tore at napkins and paper cups. When she was through, she would look at her lap as if the pieces had fallen there from the sky. Dad kept searching, even if it was in the same places that had been searched a hundred times before by a hundred different people. "We have to be missing something," he kept telling us, and finally Mom shut him up by saying sharply, "It's Aidan, Jim. We're missing *Aidan.*"

People kept coming by. They put up signs everywhere. *Missing.* That word again.

I didn't know whether it described what Aidan was or how we felt.

He was missing, and it felt like every word we spoke, every move we made, every thought we had was an act of missing him.

Think, Lucas. Think hard.

Glenn asked me if I wanted to go over to his house, to play some games. I didn't think it was his idea. I didn't want to leave, but the fact that I didn't want to leave made people think I should get out of the house.

"It'll take your mind off things," Dad said.

What he meant was that it would take their minds off of me for a second. So I went. Glenn tried to get me to play all the games Aidan would play, the ones Aidan was good at. I sucked at them because he always beat me and I always gave up. Now I was playing Aidan's games with Aidan's best friend in Aidan's best friend's house and that didn't take my mind off things at all.

"You have no idea where he is?" Glenn asked as he doused Nazis with a flamethrower.

"No," I said, not taking my eyes from the screen. "You?"

Glenn just shook his head, killed more Nazis.

When I told Glenn's mom I wanted to go back home, Glenn didn't look either disappointed or surprised.

I'd never been as much fun as my brother.

Three days turned into four days. Four days turned into five.

They wanted to dredge the pond. What if he'd fallen in? What if that was why they couldn't find him?

I noticed the difference: They weren't talking about finding Aidan. They were talking about finding Aidan's body.

My parents didn't want to hear this. When Aunt Brandi called from her vacation in Peru and told my mother she was coming home because they had to start preparing for the worst, Mom told her not to say another word, that nobody was going to talk about Aidan as if he was anything other than alive. He was missing. That's all.

I didn't think he was dead. I felt that if he were dead, I would know. The same way I'd know if one of my arms was missing or if my house had burned down. I said it to myself, "He's not dead. I know he's not dead." I made sure no one else was around when I did this.

Mom has family pictures in every room of our house. I kept looking at Aidan's face in those pictures, kept asking him where he was. I was scared that he'd be frozen in those photos forever, never getting any older.

I didn't sleep much. I listened for any sign, any signal.

I felt guilty whenever I fell asleep.

When I woke up, there were only about five seconds when I was okay, when it felt like morning on a school day. Then I'd remember what was happening, and all the fear would descend.

You're not dead, I said to him in my mind.

Then I waited for a reply.

The fifth day turned into a sixth day. The sixth day turned into a sixth night.

They expected me to go to sleep. Sleep: the scene of the crime.

Our house is two stories and an attic. Mom and Dad and some other people were downstairs. When I went to bed, everyone was trying to convince Mom to go to bed too, but she wouldn't listen. She was still down there.

I was upstairs, kept awake by every single time I'd wished to have my own room, so I wouldn't have to share one with Aidan. *This is not how I want to get it,* I told the universe, but the only response I got was from Bentley, Aidan's old teddy bear, who Mom had taken from the shelf and put back on his bed.

Bentley stared at me, as if he was telling me, *This is all your fault.*

I heard something fall. Above me. In the attic.

I don't know why I didn't call for my parents. I don't know why I didn't run downstairs.

I told myself it was the wind. A raccoon. A ghost.

But I had to know for sure.

So I walked to the end of the hall. I opened the door that's smaller than all the other doors, bent my head a little to squeeze through, and walked up the stairs.

At the top of the stairs I pulled the string that turns on the light, and the moment that bulb went on, I saw him. Aidan. On the floor, still in his pajamas. Wincing at the light. Face down, like someone had pushed him.

I said his name. He looked up at me as if my appearance was the unexpected one.

"Lucas?" he asked.

He pulled himself up. And instead of turning to face me, he looked at the tall dresser that had been hovering over his prone body, its two wooden doors spread wide like outstretched arms.

"Where is it?" he asked. "Where did it go?"

I looked over his shoulder, into the dresser. Normally it could fit dozens of hanging suits or dresses. But now . . .

"It's empty," I told him.

"No," he said. "It can't be."

"Aidan."

I said it like I had to remind him what his name was. I said it like his name would finish the job of bringing him back.

He looked the same, but also different. I saw a rip on his pajama top's right elbow that I was sure hadn't been there before. The soles of his feet were dirty. There was a leaf in his hair, and his eyes still weren't focusing on me, even though I was talking to him.

I tried again.

2

"Where were you?" I asked.

In response, he used a word I'd never heard before. He said, "Aveinieu."

3

I thought I hadn't heard him right. Or maybe he was too tired to speak clearly. I should have asked him to say it again, but instead I remembered all the people downstairs, all the people who were looking for him.

"We have to tell them you're back," I said. He didn't respond. He reached into the dresser for something that wasn't there, pressing against the back of its empty chamber. I turned from him and yelled out, "MOM! DAD! UP HERE!" I ran down the attic stairs, got to the small doorway just as they reached the hallway. "It's Aidan!" I told them. "He's back!"

They were at my heels up the stairs, then ran past me to hug Aidan, to cry, to hug him more, as if they needed to confirm that he was real, that this was real, that we were all awake. Dad pulled me into the hug and said, "You found him," which I accepted then, but immediately thought was strange, because I hadn't found him—he'd simply returned. But that didn't matter. None of the questions mattered, not at that moment. More people came up the stairs and cheered and cried and hugged Aidan like he was an organ they needed in order to breathe. He didn't say anything. He didn't cry. He looked lost, which everyone said was the shock of it, the shock of whatever had happened. *What matters is that he's back*—people said that right away and truly believed it. Someone got out their phone to let the police know. Someone else started taking pictures, saying, "You're going to want to have this recorded forever." Aidan began to shiver, and someone grabbed a blanket that was sitting on an old rocking chair. They bundled him up and the party moved downstairs.

Nobody noticed me staying behind. I wanted to be in the attic a few more minutes before anyone else came back. They were so loud downstairs—it was like every silence of the past six days had burst, and the relief was noisy because we didn't have to worry about missing someone else's shout for help underneath.

I tried to find something out of place, something that would give me a clue to how Aidan had gotten up here without any of us noticing. The attic didn't have any windows or a chimney—the only way in or out was through the small door. So he must have come back into the house, past the locked doors, past all the people downstairs, and past my open bedroom door, then up here before . . . falling on the floor and alerting me to his presence.

That was the only explanation. There was no other.

There was no way he'd been in the attic this whole time.

I turned to the dresser, wondering why Aidan had stared at it with such intensity. It had been in the attic for as long as I could remember. It had been full of old ironing boards and vacuum parts until a couple of years ago when Mom had gotten really into decluttering and had thrown all of the junk away. It had been empty ever since, and it had been empty when we'd checked it multiple times over the past six days. Just like it was empty now.

I looked. I looked closely.

There was nothing there. Absolutely nothing. Not even dust.

I closed the doors when I was done. Dad called out my name, and I heard it above all the other voices. I knew I had to go back downstairs, join the celebration.

But before I left the attic, something on the floor caught my eye.

It was the leaf. It had fallen out of Aidan's hair.

4

It was blue. Royal blue. The shape of a diamond.
I had never seen anything like it.

5

Dad called my name again. I put the leaf in my pocket, crumpling it without meaning to.

I headed downstairs.

The police came, and with them came questions. Gentle questions. Natural questions. Impossible questions.

When my parents asked Aidan where he'd been, he wouldn't answer. I could see this scared them, but I could also see he didn't have the energy left for an explanation. He looked mystified, as if he thought time wouldn't have passed while he was gone.

Everyone, even the police, made excuses. Aidan was tired. Aidan was exhausted. Aidan had been through a lot, although nobody knew exactly what. He needed to take a shower and get some sleep. There wasn't anything that couldn't wait until morning, not with him safe and sound.

I could sense that Mom didn't want to let him out of her sight. But Dad persuaded her everything was okay now.

He took a shower. He went to bed. I wanted to be there, wanted to make sure he was okay, but I was told to let him have a moment, let him rest.

Once Aidan wasn't there to be asked anything, I got asked everything instead.

How did you know he was there?

I heard a sound in the attic.

What kind of sound?

Like something falling.

Did you hear footsteps?

No.

Not Aidan walking around? Or maybe two people walking around?

No.

Lucas, you know you can't get into any trouble with us, right? We promise, you won't be in any trouble. So tell us . . . did you help Aidan get back into the house?

No.

You didn't sneak him in at any point?

No.

You had no idea he was in the attic?

Not until I saw him there.

And what did he say to you when you found him?

I think he was just . . . confused.

What do you mean?

He seemed surprised to be in the attic. He kept staring at the dresser up there.

Did you ask him where he's been?

Yes.

And what did he say?

Aveinieu.

6

The way they looked at me must have been the same way I'd looked at him.

The moment I said it, I regretted it. I had shared something that wasn't mine to share.

A-vay-nyew?

I don't know what it means. Like I said, he was very confused.

Did you ask him what he meant?

No. Because that's when I realized nobody else knew he was back. So I yelled down here.

Do you have any idea where he was?

No.

Do you have any idea how he got to the attic?

No.

Mom went to call our relatives. Dad led the police into the attic, and then they made him stay downstairs while they looked around. The people who'd been in the house went back to their own homes, telling Mom and Dad they'd call tomorrow, that they were so happy Aidan was safe.

The police were also happy Aidan was safe, but they seemed confused as well. After they searched through the attic, they came down and told Mom and Dad they'd be back in the morning to talk to Aidan, to see what he had to say. They thought I was out of earshot, but I could hear them tell my parents they needed to know if Aidan had been kidnapped, just in case the kidnapper was holding other children. But they also said that in cases like that, a kid who escapes usually raises the alarm right away. They added that, in their opinion, although Aidan seemed tired, he did not seem traumatized. I wondered how they knew the difference. Mom and Dad didn't ask.

It was after eleven by the time Mom and Dad noticed me in the kitchen, keeping out of the way. I wasn't sure if I was supposed to sleep in my room. But when Mom said, "You need to go to bed," she didn't tell me to sleep anywhere else.

I was very quiet when I stepped inside our room. But I also couldn't help myself.

"Are you awake?" I whispered.

Aidan didn't answer.

Once my eyes adjusted, I could see him in his bed, turned to the wall. I couldn't tell if he was sleeping or not.

I had no idea what he'd been through, but I knew he had to have been through *something*.

"You need to tell them where you were," I said. "Especially if other kids are in trouble."

"Nobody else is in trouble," he replied. "Let me go to sleep."

"Just promise me you won't go off again. Not like that. Otherwise, I'm going to keep waking up to check."

"I'm not going anywhere," he said, his voice sad in our bedroom darkness. "I don't think I could, even if I tried."

"What do you mean?" I asked.

But he only drew the covers higher.

"That's enough for now," he said, and I knew that was the only goodnight I would get.

I still woke up at least six different times that night. Every time I checked, he was still there.

1

Aidan got up first, but he didn't leave the bedroom until I was awake too. He was sitting on the edge of his bed, feet on the floor, facing me earnestly as I stretched and kicked off my sheets.

"I need to ask you some things," he said once I was upright.

"Okay."

"Quickly, because I think the police are already here."

"What do you want to know?"

How long was I gone?

Six days. Do you really not know?

Are you sure it was six days?

Are you kidding? Do you have any idea what's been going on here? They were searching everywhere for you.

Did they search the attic?

Yes. They searched the whole house.

And they looked inside that dresser?

Yes. Why are you asking me that? You weren't here the whole time, were you?

No, I wasn't.

Where were you?

Nobody's going to believe me.

I'll believe you.

I don't think you can.

I was about to ask him about Aveinieu, but at that moment there was a knock on our door, and Dad was asking if we were ready for breakfast.

"You can come in," Aidan said.

Dad looked like he, too, hadn't gotten much sleep; I had heard our door open and close during the night, and there were probably more check-ins I'd missed.

"Officer Ross and Officer Pinkus are here to ask you a few questions. You're not in any trouble. They—*we*—just want to know where you were, and to make sure you're okay."

"I'm fine," Aidan said.

"That's great. Truly. We just have to be sure. And, as I said, we need to know where you were."

"I can't tell you," Aidan said.

This stopped our father short.

"Now, that's the kind of answer that concerns me, Aidan. You have to be able to tell us. I assure you, you won't get into any trouble."

"It's not that I'm afraid of getting into trouble. It's just . . . you're not going to believe me."

"I promise, whatever you say, I will one-hundred-percent believe you. I know your word is good, Aidan. It always has been."

Aidan shook his head, more at something he was saying to himself than at what Dad was saying. Or at least that's how I saw it.

"Come on," Dad told him. "You'll like Ross and Pinkus. Officer Ross knew your grandfather back in the day, and Officer Pinkus is a missing persons specialist."

"I guess I was a missing person," Aidan said, getting up and heading to the door.

Dad couldn't help but pat him on the head as he walked out, saying, "Yes, Aidan. That you were."

Nobody invited me into the kitchen for the questioning, but they didn't ask me to leave either. Maybe they thought it would be easier for Aidan to talk if I was there. I hoped that was true. I wanted him to know I was on his side, whatever side that was.

Everyone but me sat at the kitchen table. I leaned against the counter, by the microwave. The detectives introduced themselves, and reassured Aidan that he wasn't in any trouble; they just needed to understand where he'd been. They started to tell him that people had been concerned about his disappearance, but Mom stepped in and corrected them, saying, "Terrified. The word for what we were is *terrified*. We were so scared, Aidan."

"I'm sorry," Aidan mumbled.

"You don't have anything to be sorry about," Dad said. Mom stayed quiet.

"Look," Officer Ross said, "this doesn't have to be a long conversation. We have a few questions, and then we can pack up and leave. In truth, it all comes down to one central question, which is: Where were you the past six days, before Lucas found you in the attic? Can you tell us that, Aidan? You can start at the beginning or wherever else you'd like."

"Nobody kidnapped me," Aidan said up front. "Nobody took me away. You don't have to worry about that."

"That's good," Officer Pinkus said carefully. "Are you saying you ran away?"

"I didn't mean to," Aidan replied.

"You got lost?" Officer Pinkus asked.

"Yes. That's definitely true."

"But where were you?" Mom broke in. "Why couldn't we find you?"

Aidan looked to the police officers instead of Mom when he asked, "Is that important? Do I really have to tell you? Isn't it enough for me to say I ran away and lost track of time where I was, but found my way back here?"

Officer Pinkus answered, "We're just trying to make sure you're okay. If you had a rough time and don't want to talk about it now, that's fine. If you'd rather talk to a counselor about it, that's fine too. But when a twelve-year-old disappears for almost a week, Aidan, we *do* need to know what happened, to help you make some sense of it. We're not here to judge you, if that's what you're afraid of. At this point, we only want to help you. I know there are a lot of people out there who are aware of your disappearance, and you don't owe any of them an explanation. This isn't about them, or me, or even your parents. This is about you."

For a moment, it was like the old Aidan was back, and wasn't in some kind of shock. I could see him get that satisfied smirk on his face, like he usually got when he found a loophole that would get him out of doing something he didn't want to do. He wasn't sarcastic with the officer—that would've been dumb. But he definitely seemed a little proud of himself when he replied, "Well, if it's about me, I'd rather not talk about it."

Officer Ross didn't look too happy about this. "Son, we turned over this whole town looking for you. A lot of people lost a lot of sleep, and your family here was scared to death. It would certainly help us to know where you were, in no small part so you'll be discouraged from running there again. Believe me when I say we do *not* want a repeat performance."

The spark of Aidan's last answer died down, and he seemed to withdraw into a more serious version of himself again. "I can't tell you," he said.

"Can't or *won't*?" Ross shot back.

Aidan didn't answer that. So Mom stepped into the silence and asked, "What—or who—is Aveinieu?"

I was facing Aidan, so I saw the effect the word had on him. It was like all the power had surged in the room, illuminating us in a brightness that was momentarily horrific, then merely blinding.

Mom went on. "Lucas told us that when he asked you yesterday where you'd been, you said *Aveinieu*."

Aidan looked to me then, confused. And I realized: He didn't remember telling me. He didn't remember it at all.

I wasn't the only one who noticed how astonished he seemed.

"Tell us, son," Officer Ross said, not unkindly. "Tell us what *Aveinieu* means."

And here Aidan said it again:

"You're not going to believe me."

8

They asked him if it was somewhere nearby. They asked him if it was a nickname. They asked him if it was a person's house. They asked him if it was a person's name. They asked him why it was a secret. Dad looked it up on his phone, but couldn't find anything. They asked Aidan again where it was, what it meant.

He tried not to tell us. He shook his head. He said it wasn't important. He swore he couldn't remember saying it to me. But I knew he was lying when he told us he didn't know what it meant, and if I knew he was lying, our parents also knew he was lying. The police officers didn't seem to understand why he was being so evasive either.

"We are not leaving this room until you tell us," Mom said.

"I can't," Aidan said. Then, "I won't."

And Mom said, "You better."

Officer Pinkus was the only one who said we didn't have to rush. "There's no reason to force the issue," she told my parents, told Aidan.

But Mom was relentless. "We thought you could be *dead*, Aidan. Do you understand that? Can you imagine how that felt? So please, just tell us where you were, so we can move on."

"I can't," Aidan said.

And I, either my brother's greatest ally or his worst betrayer, stepped over to the table and gently asked him the one question that nobody else had thought to ask.

"How did you get there, Aidan? How did you get to Aveinieu?"

It was then, only then, that Aidan gave in, revealing the one truth he knew none of us would be able to handle.

9

"The dresser," Aidan said. "I got to Aveinieu through the old dresser."

10

Officer Ross laughed.

Officer Pinkus looked concerned.

Mom said, "What?"

Dad asked, "What are you saying?"

Officer Ross said, "Very funny."

Officer Pinkus said, "I don't think he means it as a joke."

Mom asked, "What are you talking about?"

Dad said, "You're kidding, right?"

And Aidan, looking like he'd lost control of his story and was about to lose even more, said, "It's another world. They call it Aveinieu."

11

"Are you sure it's not called Narnia?" Officer Ross chuckled.

"Michael, stop," Officer Pinkus chided.

"It wasn't Narnia," Aidan said. "But it was . . . somewhere else."

"Stop, Aidan," Mom said.

"Enough," Dad warned.

"I knew you wouldn't believe me," Aidan told him. "You said you'd believe me, no matter what."

"So now you're testing me—is that what this is?" Dad asked.

I spoke up. "I don't think that's what this is."

"Not now, Lucas," Dad said. Then he turned back to Aidan. "I hope you're not finding this funny, Aidan. Because I'll tell you, none of this has been funny for us. What your mother said is true—we were terrified. And this joke of yours isn't making it any better."

"There's nothing else I can tell you," Aidan said. I think if he could have chosen to disappear again at that moment, he would have. Gratefully.

"When you say it was another world, do you mean a fantasy world or a world just like ours?" Officer Pinkus asked seriously.

"A fantasy world."

"Were there unicorns?" Officer Ross asked, not seriously.

I could tell the answer from the look on Aidan's face.

"There were unicorns, weren't there?" I said.

But nobody was listening to me.

"Please don't humor him," Mom told Officer Pinkus. "We'll never get the truth if we humor him."

Officer Pinkus took a deep breath and pushed her chair back a little.

"Aidan, Lucas," she said, "could you give me a moment with your parents? Maybe go up to your room? I'm going to ask Officer Ross to stand outside the door to the kitchen to make sure you're not eavesdropping—so please stick to your room until we come to get you, okay?"

"Okay," I said.

Without another word, Aidan stood up and left the room without me.

12

It's important to know that even though my brother was only a year older than me, he had a history of making me believe things I shouldn't have fallen for.

He told me Santa had gotten lazy, and was sending presents to our parents via Amazon. So when my parents sat me down to tell me the truth about Santa, I ended up yelling at them, "Don't lie! I know you work for him!"

He told me tooth fairies were retired dentists. It felt plausible.

He told me our grandfather had been on Normandy for D-Day. He even showed me a photo that he swore was Papa on the beach. I believed it and was so excited to talk to our dad about it, but Dad only laughed and said, "Lucas, your grandfather wasn't even born in 1944."

He told me there were monsters under the bed. Monsters in the closet. Unicorns in the backyard, but every time I went to the window, they'd magically vanished. He swore they could hear me coming. He said the only way they wouldn't sense my presence would be if I rolled my tongue. But I couldn't roll my tongue. He knew that.

All those times he'd made me a sucker were still inside me, a big ball of resentment mixed with embarrassment for falling so foolishly for whatever he'd told me. So as much as I wanted to believe him now, I also didn't want to regret believing him later.

I didn't want to fall for another story.

And this had to be a story.

I kept telling myself that.

It wasn't a question of whether it was true. I knew it wasn't. It couldn't be.

The question was:

Why was he making things up?

13

"I knew they wouldn't believe me," Aidan said when we got back to our room. "And the stupid thing is that I couldn't think of a better lie. I couldn't think of a single other place to tell them that would've worked. There are too many cameras around, you know? I couldn't just say I walked to the train station and got a train to the city— they'd check the security cameras at the station and see I was never there. Or if I said I hung out in the woods for a week—they'd ask me where, and what I lived on, and since I don't know anything about living in the woods for a week, they'd see through me in about two seconds."

"You could've said I hid you," I volunteered. "That I brought you food. They asked me that a lot."

"But why?"

"Because you needed my help?"

Aidan didn't seem convinced. "I don't mean, why would you help me. I mean, why would I leave in the first place?"

"I don't know. You tell me."

Aidan stopped and looked at me now, saw that my question wasn't about the cover story, but was about the real story instead.

"Do you really want to know?" he asked.

I nodded.

"Imagine you're up in the attic. Imagine you feel a strange wind hitting your body and then realize it's coming from the crack between the doors of the dresser. You go over to the dresser and open the doors, right? So you do that, and this dresser that's been empty for ages, that is solid wood and has nothing but a wall behind it—what if this time you open it up and instead of it being empty with a wall in the back, you see white clouds in a green sky? The wind is blowing in from that space, and when you reach your arm in, you don't hit the back of the dresser or the wall. No, you reach out into the air. And when you stick your head in, you look down and see that there's a ladder right underneath you, leading to what looks like a silver path. What do you do then? This opening has never been there before. You have no idea how long it will last. Do you step through the opening and go down the ladder or do you slam the doors shut and run for help? *You* might have run for help, Lucas. But I went down the ladder. And I'll tell you this, to answer your question: I wasn't thinking at all about leaving anything behind. I was only thinking about what I might be moving toward."

Did I believe him at that moment?

Yes. But the same way I'd believe the author of a fantasy novel I was reading. If the book is good enough, you feel like everything is true. But that doesn't mean it isn't also entirely made up.

The next thing I said was stupid.

"So when did you see the unicorns?" I asked.

I didn't mean it as a joke. I was serious. But Aidan thought I was making fun of him.

"Forget it," he said. "You wouldn't understand. And I should probably assume that anything I tell you is going to be repeated to them, anyway."

"That's not fair!" I protested.

"I should've just lied," he said. "I should have come up with a better lie."

The problem was: He'd given us a mystery to solve. And solving that mystery meant different things to each of us. For the police, it was as simple as closing a case. But for me and Mom and Dad and other people later on, it was much more personal.

For me, the mystery was confused with all the other times Aidan had lied to me, all the other times he was able to do something that I wasn't able to do. I also felt that if I were the person to solve the mystery, everybody would be really impressed with me. I would be the great detective who'd cracked it.

Which meant that when Aidan said *I should have come up with a better lie*, I heard it as him saying this whole dresser story was a lie that wasn't working, and he'd wished he'd told another lie that had worked. Even though when he'd told me about the opening and the green sky, I'd been able to imagine it was true, now I was back to wondering what the real story was, what Aidan was hiding.

Until he told the truth, he'd be getting all the attention. Unless I discovered the truth and told it first.

"Tell me what really happened," I whispered, as if all the adults were leaning against the other side of our door, listening.

41

Aidan gave me a hard stare, then reached for his phone.

"I have nothing more to say to you," he told me. Then he resumed a game he'd left off seven days before.

He didn't get much further, though. About ten minutes later, Officer Ross knocked on our door and told us to go back to the kitchen.

14

I had imagined them turning the kitchen into an interrogation room, moving the reading lamp from the den so it would shine in Aidan's face as the cops pummeled him with questions, wearing him down enough to discover where he'd buried the truth.

But instead, Officer Pinkus was already up from the table, clearly about to go. Officer Ross hung back in the doorway, looking at his watch.

"Your parents and I have had a really good talk," Officer Pinkus said once Aidan and I had sat down. "And we've all agreed that the most important thing right now is to return to normal as smoothly as possible. You and your family have been through a lot this past week—but you're back now. I am taking you at your word that you left here of your own free will, and that there wasn't anyone else involved. I can't stress enough how important it would be for you to tell us if you'd been abducted or even if you'd voluntarily gone with someone else. Is that understood?"

"Yes," Aidan said. "It was just me. I wasn't kidnapped. I didn't meet up with anyone."

Officer Pinkus nodded. "As I said, I take you at your word. But that doesn't mean you can't come to me later on if there's something more to tell. I am also taking you at your word that this won't happen again."

"It won't."

"Good. We've also agreed that you should talk to a counselor, because you have clearly been through something outside your ordinary experience. I hope you will be truthful with the counselor, because in my observation, the truth really does set you free, and allows you to go on with your life. Secrets, on the other hand, have a way of taking up all the space in the room—and you don't want that."

This time, the pause lasted a little longer than the others before Aidan realized she wanted him to say something. Then he echoed, "Yeah, I don't want that."

It didn't feel like he meant it. It felt like he was just saying what she wanted to hear.

But she took it at face value and reached out to shake Aidan's hand. He took it. As they shook, she said, "I'll come back in a few days to check in. But in the meantime, it's good to have you back."

I expected Aidan to echo again, to say, *It's good to be back*. But he didn't say anything more.

Officer Pinkus shook my hand, then Mom's and Dad's. Officer Ross was already on his way to the car.

"Have a good day," Pinkus told us.

Then she left us alone, and none of us knew what to do next.

15

It was a Thursday. All our friends were at school. Most of their parents were at work.

We were marooned at our kitchen table.

Mom had never been a good fake. If she was annoyed with you, you knew she was annoyed. Most of the time, the only question was what had spurred the annoyance. Did you leave the refrigerator door open? The toilet seat up? Did you use the last toilet paper and not replace the roll? Were you trying to watch YouTube before your homework was finished?

In this case, it was obvious that Mom had a lot to say on the subject of Aidan's disappearance and the story he'd told the police. But it was also obvious that she thought she was doing a good job of hiding this and appearing calm. I was sure Aidan could see the strain. He'd been on the receiving end of Mom's exasperation many more times than I had. He knew its language even better than I did.

If she was going to play calm, he was going to play along.

Dad usually liked to paper over the serious moments with jokes. But his mind wasn't kicking into joke mode right now—probably because all the jokes would lead to him making fun of Aidan's story.

So we did what most families do when conversation is impossible: We ate. Mom offered to make eggs, but I said cereal was fine and Aidan agreed. He didn't eat much, though. I saw him trying, but it also looked like trying, not eating. I wondered what was going on with that. When I was done eating and Aidan was done trying to eat, Dad told us he might go to the office. None of us objected. Mom said she'd work at home. About a second after she said that, the phone rang—Aunt Brandi, home now from Peru, calling for an update.

"One sec," Mom said, then moved to another room so we wouldn't hear her.

Dad got his stuff together and looked for any new objections before he headed out the door. Then he left me and Aidan alone in the kitchen. Aidan spotted something on the counter, went over to get it, then brought it back to the table.

It was one of the missing posters.

Aidan pondered his own photo and the plea for help beneath.

"I guess it was a big deal, huh?" he said. "Like, the kids at school will know about it?"

"Uh, yeah," I told him. "Pretty much everyone in the county knew about it. And most of them were looking for you."

"Ugh. What a mess."

I was annoyed with him then, and I wasn't going to hide it like my parents were hiding it.

"Yeah, *what a mess*," I repeated sarcastically. "Isn't it a bummer that you're going to have to deal with the fact that everyone stopped what they were doing in order to find you before it was, you know, *too late*? Such a shame that while you were riding unicorns or petting dragons or whatever, they were dredging the pond to look for your body and checking every single corner of this town for you. Sucks, right? The police kept asking me and Glenn questions we didn't know how to answer, and each time, we had to wonder whether giving the wrong answer was going to lead to you never being found. What a mess! But hey—I guess this can be a learning experience for every-one. In particular, next time you go into a fantasy world? Do us a favor and *leave a note*."

Aidan stood up then, rinsed out his cereal bowl, and put it in the dishwasher.

"You're never going to understand," he told me when he was done. "But that's fine. I'd never expect you to. So let's just follow everyone's lead and pretend it's a normal day, okay? Did anyone get my homework assignments while I was gone? I might as well catch up before I go back tomorrow."

"Our teachers emailed our assignments for the past few days."

"You didn't go to school either?" Aidan looked surprised by this.

"Clearly I'm not the only person who's never going to understand," I said.

Then I left him alone with his missing poster.

16

I wasn't sure whether it was deliberate or not, but a lot of the time that day, when Mom was on the phone, we could hear what she said. People were calling to see how Aidan was, how all of us were doing. And once Mom told them we were fine, doing well, the natural next thing was for them to ask her what had happened, if the mystery had been explained.

"We're just focusing on the present," she'd tell the person on the other end of the phone, whether they were a relative, a neighbor, or a friend.

From Mom's end of the conversation, it was clear that most people were okay to stop there. But a few persisted. I imagined them saying, *You don't have to tell us what happened—just tell us where he was. We looked so hard for him. Where did we miss?* Because Mom's answers were:

"It's complicated."

"No, he wasn't anywhere we thought to look."

"No, it was just him. Nobody else. He was on his own the whole time."

And, most often, "We're just happy to have him back." Over and over again.

I could hear her from the bedroom and I was sure Aidan could hear her from the den.

There were also Dad's calls, checking in. "They're doing homework," she told him. "It's like nothing happened."

But that didn't make any sense. The fact that Aidan was quietly doing homework was total evidence that something was off. Ordinarily on a day home from school he'd be texting his friends nonstop—they had this game they'd play where three of them would email a word at the same time, and then they'd Google the three words together—*badger Halloween cloud,* for example—and see what the funniest result was, usually a really weird video. Or he'd find a multiplayer game where he could dial in and stave off zombies with other players from time zones where school wasn't in session, whether it was Tokyo or Berlin. At the very least, he couldn't sit for more than an hour without getting up for a snack, usually stopping by wherever I was to mess with me.

But Aidan didn't want to talk to me now, or to anyone else. He didn't even snack.

Couldn't Mom see that?

I kept waiting for Aidan to sneak up to the attic. I left my door open in hope of catching him.

When he didn't go up there, I went myself. Walked to the dresser. Felt for a wind. Opened the doors and found nothing but air and wood. Closed the doors. Opened them again. Pretended to walk away, then quickly turned back and opened them a third time.

Nothing. Just a dresser.

When I got back to our room, Aidan was there, getting some books from his backpack.

"Find anything?" he asked casually.

"Nope," I told him.

He went back downstairs.

The only person who asked to talk to me and Aidan on the phone was Aunt Brandi. Mom passed it over to me first, then left me alone when I made it clear I wasn't going to talk until she stopped hovering.

"How's it going over there?" Aunt Brandi asked.

"Great," I said. It was kind of an automatic response.

"Is that so?" Aunt Brandi's low voice didn't seem to believe me. "I know you're excited to have Aidan back, but I can't imagine it's an easy time."

"It's okay."

"Mom told me where Aidan says he was. That must be a lot to take in."

"It doesn't really matter what he says, as long as he's back."

"Of course. But it's okay to think it's a little strange. You know that, right?"

"Sure."

"And are your parents behaving themselves?"

This was something that Aunt Brandi always asked me when she called.

"Well, Mom's mad and Dad's at work."

"That's my assessment too. Listen, Lucas—will you do me a favor? Can you take care of your brother and try to help him out however you can? I'll come down over the weekend to help out too, because no matter what Aidan says, he's going to need us in his corner now. Especially with you going back to school tomorrow."

"There's no way of getting out of it, I guess."

"Nope—school's the plan. But, believe me, that's much better than sitting around on pause for any longer. Anyway, can I talk to Aidan? Is he there with you?"

"I'll go get him."

"Thanks, Lucas. You know where to reach me, anytime."

I walked down to the den and passed the phone over to

Aidan. Just like I hadn't really started talking until Mom left, he didn't really talk until I left.

I wondered if Aunt Brandi would be able to get the truth out of him. She was Mom's youngest sister by a stretch, halfway in age between Mom and us. She lived in the city and worked as a graphic designer for a T-shirt company. This meant Aidan and I were always getting free T-shirts with random slogans—my favorite was a penguin standing in the middle of a crowded street asking, "Where can I get some ice?" while Aidan loved one that showed a snail trying to swipe a phone twice its size.

"Did you have a good talk?" Mom called out from the study before I could get back to my room.

I poked my head in. "Yeah. She said we're going back to school tomorrow."

Mom nodded. "I don't see why not."

"Even though it's Friday?"

"Last time I checked, there was still school on Fridays. And you and Aidan have missed enough already. Your teachers can catch you up tomorrow so you won't be so behind next week."

She started asking me about homework, and I was going through it class by class when Aidan barged in, the phone still in his hand.

He glared at our mom. "I can't believe you told her! Why did you tell her?"

"Because she's my sister and I tell her everything."

"But that's mine! Aveinieu is *mine*. You even told her its name!"

"Why does that matter? She's not going to tell anyone. And, quite honestly, I needed her opinion, because I don't quite know what to do with your story, Aidan. Until you tell us what really happened, I'm at something of a loss. Officer Pinkus told us to be patient with you, and we will be. I know that whatever happened, it had to have been a lot. And the last thing I want is for you to disappear again. If you don't want to let us in, that's fine. But this is something your dad and I and Lucas are going through too. And we need to do what we have to in order to navigate it. For me, that means talking to Brandi. I'm not going to be telling your story to the mailman or your teachers or even your grandparents. The last thing I want is for anyone else to hear it."

Mom had just thrown a lot at him, but there was only one thing Aidan caught.

"So you don't believe me?" he said.

Mom took a deep breath. "It's just very hard to believe, Aidan. But if it's the story you want to tell, I'll support that. I'm only worried—we're all worried—that there's something underneath that you're trying to hide. And it will be much better for you to let it come to the surface, so we can deal with it together."

Before, if Mom called Aidan on something, he would match her attack with one of his own. If she tried to pin him down with a sentence, he'd use a sentence to get out of it. If she tried to pile on a paragraph, he'd build his own paragraph and push it over to her. So I was expecting him to really let go of some words now, to say something like, *If you really want some things to come to the surface, let me show you the thoughts that are coming up right now.*

But instead, "It's the truth" was all he said. Then he handed the phone to me and went back to the den.

I passed the phone to my mother, who also looked like she'd been expecting more back from Aidan. That was how they connected.

Now she asked me, "I'm not off base, am I?" Then, realizing who she was talking to, she walked it back. "Never mind. We've all been under a lot of strain. Brandi said to keep that in mind, and to make allowances."

"Are you sure that includes going back to school tomorrow?"

This got a half smile from Mom, which under the circumstances counted as a full smile.

"Yes. It does."

We pretty much stayed in our separate rooms until three o'clock. Then Mom caught Aidan making a move for the front door. I could hear them from our bedroom.

"Where do you think you're going?" Mom asked.

"To Glenn's. School's over. He texted that he's home."

"You aren't going anywhere. He can come here another day. You're grounded for the near future—you are *not* to leave this house without an adult around."

"Not even to Glenn's?"

"Not even to Glenn's."

"That's not fair!"

"I'm not sure you get to be the judge of fair and not fair right now, Aidan."

"Fine!"

Aidan's footsteps stomped toward me, and soon he was back in the room. I pretended to be doing my homework.

He wasn't fooled.

"I assume you heard all that?" he said.

"Mmm-hmm."

"I guess I'm a prisoner here."

I didn't point out that we'd all been prisoners for six days while he was gone. Instead I said, "It doesn't make much sense anyway."

"Yeah. What would happen if I went to Glenn's house?"

"No, I mean, what's the point of grounding you and keeping you here if the way you get out is up in the attic?"

"That's not funny."

"It wasn't meant to be funny. It was meant to be, like, logical."

"It's not going to open up again."

This intrigued me. "How do you know?"

Instead of elaborating, Aidan said, "I just know."

Then he left the room.

It felt like Mom spent the afternoon on the phone. "He hasn't told us anything yet," she kept saying. "He hasn't told us anything at all."

At around five, Aidan went up to the attic. But he was back down in two minutes and gave me a dirty look for checking up on him.

Dad came home. We had dinner. I thought we were supposed to be acting like everything was normal, but it didn't feel normal. Aidan wouldn't talk or eat. Dad and

Mom kept looking at him. They didn't pay any attention to me. The mystery filled the room so much that it was hard to breathe.

Aidan was no longer missing, but now it was like the answers to his disappearance were missing instead.

17

Aidan and I didn't say much the whole night. Then we were in our room and the lights were out and both of us were there in bed, trying to sleep and not sleeping. Sharing a room, this was often the space for us to let off what was on our minds, what might keep us awake or simply what we needed to tell someone else before we forgot it the next day. Usually it was Aidan who spoke up, whether because he had more to say or because he needed an audience more. Sometimes he'd just be telling me about something he and his friends had found online. ("Did you know that some people dress up their pet badgers for Halloween?") Or maybe he'd be venting about some injustice, online or off. ("There are three guys in this house and only one Mom, so I don't see why, statistically, it makes sense for us to have to put down the toilet seat every single time after we pee. Especially in *our* bathroom.") Mostly my job was to laugh or to agree.

This time I knew he wouldn't be the one to start things off. When a thought came into my mind, I almost left it there. But I was curious, and the curiosity spread to my tongue. There in the darkness, it was easier for curiosity to take over.

"Did they speak English?" I found myself asking Aidan, although I made it sound like I was asking the air.

"What?" he asked back, even though it was pretty obvious what I meant.

"In Aveinieu. Did they speak English? That's what I've never understood about most books where people from our world go into a fantasy world. All of the creatures in the fantasy world speak English. That seems too convenient."

Was I asking this to make fun of his story? Was I asking in order to catch him in a lie, to make him explain things until he contradicted himself and proved himself to be a liar? Or was I simply curious about how it all had worked for him, back in Aveinieu? There's no clear motive, except for this: Sometimes we ask questions because we hope the answers will tell us why we asked the question in the first place.

He could've blown me off. He could've told me to shut up. Maybe because we were in the dark, maybe because we weren't looking at each other, he did something else instead.

He told me more of the story, and made it sound like the truth.

"The Aveinieu didn't speak English, or any other language someone from our world would know. But I wasn't the only person from our world there. There was this older woman, Cordelia, who'd lived there since she was my age. So for fifty years or so. And she'd learned how to talk to them. She was the one who found me, and she became my translator. She tried to explain it all to me."

"How long were you there?"

"I don't know. Their days and nights aren't like ours. But probably a month?"

"And did you live with Cordelia?"

"Yeah. She took a lot of us in. The ones from our world."

"How many of you were there?"

"Seven or eight."

"Which one—seven or eight?"

"What is this, a quiz? Forget I said anything, okay? Forget all of it."

"Come on! Tell me more."

"Why? So you can tell Mom and Dad?"

"I won't tell anyone."

"You better not. Especially at school tomorrow. Do you understand?"

I imagined the reaction I'd get if I tried to explain to my friends what Aidan said had happened.

"Do you really think I'd tell anyone?"

"All I'm saying is, you better not. Now stop asking me questions. I need to go to bed."

I should have left it there. But I wasn't sure I'd ever get him to talk again. So I said, "Can I ask one last question?"

"What?"

"Why did you come back?"

For a while I didn't think he was going to answer. Then, right before I fell asleep, I heard him say, "It wasn't my choice."

18

Normally, Aidan and I took the bus to school. I'd assumed that was how we were going to get there on the first day back. But instead, Mom and Dad informed us over breakfast that they'd both be taking us to school—and coming in with us, to meet with the principal and the guidance counselor.

"That's not embarrassing or anything," Aidan mumbled.

"If you were worried about being embarrassed, you should've thought twice before you—" Dad started. But he couldn't—wouldn't—finish the sentence. It was like he didn't want to mention the possibility of Aveinieu out loud.

None of us finished the sentence for him.

I guess we didn't want to talk about it either.

"My teachers, the principal, the guidance counselor—you haven't told any of them what happened, have you?" Aidan asked on the way over.

Both of our parents looked at him in the rearview.

"No," Mom said. "And nobody's supposed to ask. They're supposed to leave you alone."

Aidan looked relieved. But I thought: *Who wants to be alone?*

Principal Kahler was grinning like a military general who'd just won a battle. As if to balance him out, Mr. Lemon, our guidance counselor, looked like he was trapped on an icy lake and the temperature was starting to rise into the nineties.

"We had an assembly yesterday," the principal told Aidan, "and in addition to celebrating your return, we also warned the student body that our no-tolerance policy extends to anyone who doesn't respect your privacy in this difficult time. No one is to put you on the spot, make you feel uncomfortable, or treat you any differently than they would have treated you if you'd been in school this past week. And, frankly, that applies to the teachers as well as the students. If anything happens, you have permission to come straight to me or Mr. Lemon. In return we expect you to resume your studies and continue to be a valued member of our middle school community. Does that sound like a good deal to you?"

"Yes," Aidan replied. Principal Kahler was, I thought, being really nice, but Aidan still looked like he was getting detention.

"You and I will get to talk fifth period," Mr. Lemon added. "I've already arranged it with Ms. Simon."

I could see that Aidan wanted to groan out, "Oh, great." But he held it in.

"That's very generous of you," Mom said. As if it wasn't Mr. Lemon's job.

The first bell rang. Principal Kahler stood up to shake our hands.

"Let's see how this goes," he said.

Glenn was waiting for Aidan outside the main office. Mom and Dad looked happy to see him. Aidan looked embarrassed.

"Heya," Glenn said.

"What's up?" Aidan said back.

"Not much." Glenn smiled. "You?"

Aidan shrugged. "Not much."

"Cool."

"Cool."

Then they walked off without giving the rest of us another look.

This left me with Mom and Dad.

"Promise you'll call us if anything goes wrong," Dad said.

"Uh, sure," I promised. I was a little curious what Dad meant by "wrong"—Aidan running away from school? Bullies bullying his story out of him? Unicorns invading fifth period in order to get him back? But I also knew if I asked for clarification, I'd probably end up talking to them past the late bell, and I really wanted to get to homeroom and have my regular life begin again.

"Bye!" I said so loud and cheery it probably looked like I was auditioning for the school musical.

While I walked through the hallway, I could see a few people looking at me, but not too many. My best friends, Busby and Tate, found me while I was at my locker. Although they'd offered to have me over to their houses, I hadn't really talked to them while Aidan was missing. Now I could see they were torn between playing it cool and asking me everything.

It was Busby who broke first, her voice barely a whisper.

"Are you okay?" she asked. "I mean, is Aidan okay? I know we're not supposed to ask where he was . . . but I can ask if you're okay, right?"

"And if you happen to want to tell us where he was, we won't argue," Tate added with a grin.

"We're not really talking about that," I said apologetically.

"No worries," Busby said quickly. "At all. Everyone's just glad he's okay."

Tate nodded. "Yeah. Both my mom and dad were part of the crew looking for him."

"Mine too," Busby said.

"So, yeah . . . we're all just glad he came back."

This would happen to me over and over throughout the day—kids telling me how their parents had looked for Aidan. Even some of the teachers told me they'd been part of the search parties. Other kids told me how much they'd prayed for Aidan's return. Everyone said how glad they were that he was home safe . . . but I could tell that at least some of them were expecting more from me than thanks. They wanted to know what had happened. They felt they were owed an explanation. And I had nothing to give them.

Busby laid off at lunch, but Tate and another friend of ours, Truman, were relentless.

"You don't have to tell us," Truman said. "But if we guess right, throw a French fry our way."

Then they started guessing.

"He ran away to Disney World."

"He was abducted by Ms. Holt for science experiments."
(Ms. Holt was our not-particularly-friendly bio teacher.)

"He was abducted by aliens."

"He's been an alien all along and needed to visit his real parents in a galaxy far, far away."

"Two words: *time travel.*"

"Two more words: *witness protection.*"

I kept my French fries to myself, and hoped hard that my friends wouldn't actually guess Aidan's story, because if they'd said, "He went into another world, like Narnia," I wasn't sure I could keep my expression neutral.

But they never got near it.

Eventually Busby told them to cut it out, and changed the conversation to weekend plans.

I gave her a few French fries in thanks.

19

Although I was thinking about Aidan all the time during school, I didn't see him until the end of the day. Once again, we weren't taking the bus—Mom had given us instructions on where and when to meet her, and she backed those up with a series of texts.

I met Aidan by his locker, which had been decorated with balloons and streamers, as if it was his birthday or he'd won a big prize.

He saw me looking at them and said, "They also made a big 'welcome back' banner for my homeroom. Ms. Geller made a really big deal about it. She gave this speech about how good it was to have me back. Then she made the whole class applaud and cheer. It was mortifying."

"Was it better after that?"

Aidan did the combination for his locker and accidentally popped a balloon when he swung it open. "Not much.

I think whatever Principal Kahler said to them in the assembly only made them more curious. For the most part, they left me alone . . . but I could tell they didn't want to."

"Yeah, I got that too."

He stared at me hard. "But you didn't say anything, right?"

"Of course I didn't say anything."

Aidan's stare moved over my shoulder. I turned and found Glenn hovering there.

"Bad time?" he asked.

"Nah," Aidan said, taking the last of the books from his locker and closing it fast enough that another balloon fell off. "Mom's picking us up."

"Cool. I'll see you tomorrow, right?"

"Right."

"Even though you're grounded?" I asked.

Aidan looked annoyed with me. "Grounded means I can't leave the house. It doesn't mean Glenn can't come over."

I wasn't sure about that—but I figured we'd find out soon enough. Neither of us had been grounded before. Not like this.

"Yeah, what do *you* know?" Glenn chimed in scornfully. Which I thought was unnecessary.

"I know more than you do," I shot back, regretting it immediately.

"Stop," Aidan said to me. Then he smiled at Glenn and said, "We'll definitely hang out tomorrow. Just show up."

"Cool. See ya."

"See ya."

Aidan started walking to our pickup point. Kids kept stopping him to say welcome back and that they were glad he was okay. Some girls even told him how scared they'd been when he'd been missing—I couldn't tell if they were friends of his or not. He wasn't unfriendly to anyone, but he also made it clear he didn't want to talk about it. He kept walking. I kept following.

The phones buzzed in our pockets at the same time. Mom, already there. Mom, waiting.

When we got in the car, she asked the usual question— "How was your day?"—but it felt more loaded than usual. As if to confirm that, she added before we'd even answered, "And how did the talk with the counselor go?"

"It was fine," Aidan mumbled from the back seat.

From the front seat, I could see that this answer wasn't good enough for Mom.

"Aidan," she said, trying to keep her voice light and only half succeeding, "when you disappear for six days, you forfeit the right to give brief, unhelpful answers. So let's try again. What did you and the counselor talk about?"

"We talked about my 're-entry' into school. Since I'd

only been in school for four periods, I told him I was 're-entering' fine. He asked me if there was anything else I wanted to talk about, from when I'd been 'away.' I told him I didn't. He went on for another ten minutes about how he was there for me if I needed him. I told him that was great. Is that a good enough report for you?"

"Why didn't you want to talk to him more about it?"

"He's a guidance counselor, Mom. He's not a psychiatrist."

"Would you like to speak to a psychiatrist? Your father and I have gotten some names and are trying to get you an appointment for Monday."

"Are you asking me or not asking me? It's kinda unclear."

Mom did *not* like that response.

"Again, Aidan, I'll point out that you forfeited some say in what happens when you ran away for so long and caused so much pain and worry. If I were you, I'd stop the arguing right here, right now."

"I'm not arguing," Aidan said flatly. Which seemed to me a lot like arguing, but I wasn't going to point that out.

Mom let out a deep breath, then turned to me.

"How was your day, Lucas?"

I really had to stop myself from saying, "It was fine." Instead I gave her a play-by-play of daily life in Roanoke, which was what we were studying in American history. This lasted long enough to get us home without Mom and Aidan arguing anymore.

When we got to the house, Aidan bolted from the back seat and headed inside before I'd even undone my seat belt. I figured he was running to our room, but when I got there, I found it empty. Instead there were footsteps over my head. He'd run to the attic.

I stood still, listening. What would I do if the footsteps suddenly stopped? It sounded like he was going to the dresser. I could imagine him opening the doors, and then—

The footsteps pounded back down the stairs. A few seconds later, Aidan was in our room, looking angry.

"Find anything?" I asked.

"Shut up," he said.

"Don't take it out on me if they don't want you back," I said.

A direct hit.

"You don't understand me at all," he swore.

But from his reaction, I could tell I'd understood at least a little bit of what he'd been hoping for up there.

20

Dinner was strained. Dad asked the same questions about school that Mom had, and got the same answers (except a little less about Roanoke from me). Aidan again made a weird face when he tried to eat, like the turkey and stuffing were poisoned but the executioner was insisting he eat it all.

"I think it will be great for you to talk to Dr. Jennings on Monday," Dad said. "He's a smart guy."

"If that's a part of my prison sentence, fine," Aidan replied.

"You are not in prison," Mom pointed out. "You are home. Being grounded means you're home."

"Whatever," Aidan said. I really didn't think he was helping himself out. He usually knew when to stop, but now it was like he didn't care whether he crossed lines or not.

Dad put out a hand toward Mom, signaling her not to say whatever he knew she'd want to say next. He leaned over to look Aidan right in the eye.

"Look, buddy, you've gotta help us out here, okay? Everyone was super nice to us when you were gone, and they're being super respectful now that you're back. Everyone wants you to get beyond this. It would help us to know a little more. Right now, all we have is your story . . . and that's not much to go on."

Aidan looked at the table. "It isn't a story."

"But it *is* a story, Aidan. We all know that. If it's the story you need to tell, we understand. But at the end of the day, we all know it's a story, and stories always have some meaning behind them. We're just trying to get to the meaning, bud. That's all."

"I told you . . . it's not a story."

It struck me right then that the word *story* might be too big for us. Because the same word could be used for something that had happened and something that was completely made up. Me telling my parents what happened in school, sticking totally to the facts, was a story. But me telling them I'd spent the school day on Mars would also be a story. It was tricky, the way it could mean both things.

"Aidan," Mom said gently, "you're not making this

easy . . . especially for yourself. That's why we want you to talk to Dr. Jennings."

"I didn't say I wouldn't," Aidan pointed out, looking up again.

"Well, that's good!" Dad said cheerily.

We didn't go near the topic of Aveinieu again.

21

Once more, I waited until the lights were out and the house had fallen silent. I waited until the hour when we were still awake but had already let go of the day. Waiting for sleep to come . . . and having some words arrive instead.

"What was it like there?" I asked from my bed.

He could have pretended to be asleep. He could have told me to stop it already—I wouldn't have been surprised by that.

But instead he asked, "What do you mean?"

"I mean, what was it like in Aveinieu? Were there cities? Castles? Shires?"

"It wasn't like any of that. There weren't many people— like, people weren't the point of everything. There weren't any roads or electricity or things like that. People didn't even ride horses—not unless the horse offered its back, which it only did when there were emergencies. We had to walk everywhere. I lived in a wood cabin that Cordelia and some of the others had built."

"There wasn't any electricity?"

"Nope."

"Why didn't you, like, invent it for them?"

"Would you know how to invent electricity?"

I thought about it for a second. I didn't have a clue how electricity worked, or how it got into the sockets.

"I guess not," I admitted.

"But there were toilets. Plumbing. It was all from tanks that caught the rain."

"Phew."

"But no toilet paper, of course."

"Of course."

I waited for him to tell me something else. When he didn't, I asked another question.

"Were there other kids?"

"You mean, human kids?"

"Yeah."

"There were a few. There was one kid a couple years older than me who was from our world. His portal was in China—he didn't speak any English and I didn't speak any Mandarin, but luckily one of Cordelia's friends spoke both. So we figured out how to talk. He was a little freaked out because the weather was really warm, and he was from somewhere really cold. I mean, he was freaked out about other things too. Like the maddoxes."

"The maddoxes?"

"We don't have them here. They're, like, part bear and part ox. It's hard to explain. There were a lot of creatures like that. Honestly, I only saw about one percent of all the creatures they have in Aveinieu. We didn't travel that far."

"Why not?"

I could hear Aidan turn over in his bed to face me.

"Because it was just life," he said. "There wasn't any quest. There wasn't any treasure to find or secret to unlock. It was like living on a farm, only the farm happened to be in a completely different world."

"I thought you didn't like farms!"

"This wasn't a third-grade field trip to see some cows and goats, Lucas. It was so weird. All the colors were off—Cordelia said it might be our eyes, and that the light just hit them a different way. But there was a green sky and a silver sun and these trees that were—"

"Blue," I said, suddenly remembering the leaf that had been in his hair.

Aidan turned on the lamp next to his bed.

"Why did you say that?" he asked.

I was already up, digging through my hamper for the pajama bottoms I'd been wearing two nights ago.

"There was a leaf in your hair!" I said as I dug. "I put it in my pocket."

The pajamas were now in my hand, and I reached into the pocket and felt the crushed leaf in my fingers. Even before I pulled it out, I could tell it was now in pieces.

Aidan was up and next to me. "Let me see," he said. "Give it over."

I cupped the remnants in my hand, then offered them to him.

He and I saw it at the same time:

Not only was the shape destroyed, but the blue leaf had turned . . . brown.

It looked like any other leaf.

"No," Aidan said. *"No."*

We stared at the pieces in my hand.

"I swear, it was blue when I picked it up. And shaped kind of like a diamond. Here."

I put the remains of the leaf in his hands. I didn't know what else to do with them. And now he didn't know what to do with them either.

"This is all that's left, then," he said sadly.

"It's something, right?" I offered.

"Is it?" he said, putting the brown pieces in his top desk drawer, then shutting it.

"I'm sorry I didn't put it somewhere safe. A lot was going on."

He got back into bed and turned out the light.

"It's okay," he said. "It wouldn't have mattered."

Maybe he was right. But I still felt bad.

"Tell me about some of the other colors," I said when I got back into my bed.

"Nah. I need to go to sleep."

So we stopped there.

He didn't ask me if I believed him now. Which was good, because I still didn't know what to believe. Maybe in all the excitement, I'd been wrong about the leaf. Now it just seemed like a normal, broken leaf.

It no longer had any story to tell.

22

True to his word, Glenn showed up at ten o'clock the next morning. Mom and Dad clearly hadn't talked about whether a visit would be against the rules, and once Glenn was there, they weren't about to chase him off. I followed Aidan and Glenn down to the den, but they positioned themselves on the couch in a way that made it obvious I wasn't wanted. And then, just in case I didn't get the point, Aidan said, "It's a two-player game, Lucas."

I went upstairs to get my homework—there was still a lot left over from the week we'd missed. Then I made a space for myself behind the couch. Glenn and Aidan knew I was there, but as long as I wasn't in their way, that was fine.

Usually when Aidan and Glenn played two-player games, it was a very loud sport. They loved making up insult jokes for each other—"My grandma drinks tea better than you shoot zombies!" "You're steering that car like it's a half-wheeled bicycle!" "I've seen better hand-eye coordination in ticklish sloths!" It was like their commentary about the game was as fun as the game itself. But now . . . mostly I heard the sounds of the game. At one point, Glenn yelled out, "I crush you like an ant with my clown shoes!" but Aidan didn't have a response. I figured Glenn was letting him take the lead. Then, after about an hour of them playing, I heard Glenn say, casually, "So, dude . . . where were you?"

I made myself really still, because I knew if my presence was felt, Aidan might not answer.

The game sounds continued. Finally, Aidan asked, "Does it matter?"

Glenn laughed. "Of course it matters! It's all anyone can talk about! And since I have, you know, best friend status, they're asking me all the time. Not that I'd tell them, right? But a guy's gotta ask."

Aidan tried a joke, but it sounded forced. "You afraid that they implanted a supercomputer in my brain, which is why I'm beating you so badly at this game?"

"How'd they get a supercomputer in there?" Glenn bantered back. "Oh yeah, there was all that extra space from you missing a brain." Then he steered back to the original question. "Seriously, I'm dying to know."

Aidan hedged. "I'm really not telling anyone. That's what the police wanted."

"But you can tell me."

Tell him, I thought. Glenn wanted to know so badly . . . and if Aidan couldn't tell him, then I knew he wouldn't be able to tell anyone else.

Aidan kept playing the game. As he did, he said, "I don't know what to tell you. I don't remember a lot of it. They think I must have been sleepwalking or something. But I left the house and walked into the woods and got completely lost. I must've been walking and walking. Even after I woke up, I had no idea where I was. Eventually I found this cabin, but no one was home. I found a key under the front mat and let myself in. It didn't have electricity or anything, and barely had food. I didn't feel good and I must've been really sick, because I completely lost track of time. I must've had the worst fever, but there wasn't any way to call for help. So I just stayed there until I was strong enough to leave. I walked for a while and eventually got to Route 95—I was afraid to get into a stranger's car, so I just walked in the woods alongside the highway until I knew where I was. Then I made it home. I left a note in the cabin and I'm hoping they'll call here, so I can figure out where I was. But I don't think it was close."

The game paused—I had to assume it was Glenn who'd done the pausing.

"That's crazy!" he said. "Like, really crazy!"

"I know, right?" Aidan said. "If it hadn't happened to me, I wouldn't believe it."

"I had no idea you sleepwalked!"

"This was the first time. I think Mom and Dad are bolting all the doors now, just in case."

Glenn whistled, and I could hear him lean back on the couch. "And here we were, looking all over town for you. But you weren't even in town."

"Nope. I wish I remembered walking that much, but I really don't."

"Dude, that sucks."

"I know. Can we keep playing?"

"Sure."

The game sounds resumed.

I wanted Aidan's new story to make more sense. And as far as it stuck to the real world, it definitely made more sense than Aveinieu. Route 95 existed much more than any place that included unicorns and maddoxes. So that should have made it much more believable.

But the truth?

Aidan sounded more truthful when he was talking about Aveinieu. I obviously couldn't see his face from behind the couch, but something was missing in his voice when he was explaining it to Glenn—Dad would have called it *sincerity*. Aidan didn't sound like he really meant it.

I also didn't believe that a sleepwalker could make it

that far without leaving a trace. Or that he could spend six days wandering without his pajamas getting that messy. Or that no one spotted him at any point on his way home. Or that he could make it back into our locked house un-detected. Or that he found a cabin without any electricity and without any neighbors so close to our suburb.

So what you're saying is that you think your brother went into a fantasy world? I asked myself.

Well, maybe there's another option. Maybe neither one of the stories is true.

"How are you guys doing?"

My concentration was broken by the sight of Dad in the doorway, checking up on us.

"Good," Aidan said.

"Great," Glenn seconded.

Then Dad looked at me behind the couch. "Lucas?"

"Just working."

Glenn peered over the couch at me. "Dude! I forgot you were there!"

Dad laughed at that.

"Alright, guys," he said, "you can't spend the whole day playing video games. I'll come back in an hour or so to break for lunch, and then Glenn's going to have to go home so Aidan can get some of his homework done. If he gets enough done, you can come back tomorrow. Just call first, okay?"

"Will do," Glenn said.

As soon as Dad left, I expected Aidan to tell me to leave. But he didn't say anything, so I stayed. I waited for Glenn to ask him more, but he didn't.

I guessed this meant he was satisfied with Aidan's answer.

I wasn't.

23

After lunch, Glenn went home and Aidan went to our room to do homework. Mom asked me if I wanted to go to the grocery store with her, and I said sure. For the past week, we'd been mostly eating meals people brought over. It was time to eat our own food again.

Usually we bumped into one or two people at the grocery store, but this time it was like a group text had gone out, and in every aisle there was someone else to hug Mom or smile at Mom or tell Mom how glad they were that Aidan was home. Mom was polite about all the attention but she didn't really welcome it. I barely recognized anybody who was talking to us, and a few even looked at me and asked, "Is that him?"

No, I wanted to say, *I'm the other one.* But instead I left it to Mom to correct them.

"Let's make this as quick as possible," Mom told me

during a clear minute. We zoomed through as best as we could—but had to stand there awkwardly while Minnie, the checkout person we always went to, cried and told us how her prayers had been answered.

Because I'd stayed at home most of the time Aidan had been gone, I hadn't realized how *involved* everyone else felt.

And if *I* didn't know it, I was pretty sure Aidan didn't know it either.

Dinner that night was almost normal.

Mom cooked. Aidan set the table. Dad and I were in charge of dessert.

We didn't talk about Aveinieu.

Instead, Mom talked a little about the people in the grocery store. And Dad talked about how everyone at work was also so glad. Aidan kept moving the food around on his plate, nearly choking when he tried Mom's corn bread, which wasn't great but wasn't *that* bad. Dad changed the subject to the World Series, and what he expected to happen in the game that night. We talked about baseball the whole time, the only awkward moment coming when Dad mentioned an injury that had happened to one of the players while Aidan was away.

After the table was cleared and chores were finished,

we watched the Series together in the den. I thought that anyone looking in our window would have seen a regular family watching a baseball game. Mom and Dad might have looked at Aidan a little more than usual. I might have as well, as if I continued to need proof he was back. But that was the only thing different, and that was barely noticeable.

For a while, I let myself believe it was all going to be okay.

24

Near midnight, bedroom darkness.

"What did you eat there?" I asked.

Aidan didn't say, *Stop asking me questions. I was in a cabin off the highway the whole time.* He didn't say, *It's none of your business.* Or even, *Let me go to sleep.*

Instead, he said, "It was mostly things we grew. No meat, out of respect for the other creatures. It wasn't like here, where there's a hierarchy—you know, people in control and then animals on the farm to be eaten. Or pets. It's not like that. So instead of, like, burgers, we had a lot of vegetables. Some of them were ones I knew, like corn. But others—I had no idea what I was eating. I just had to trust that I wasn't allergic or something."

"What was your favorite?"

"They have this food called gak—it's like the most intense corn bread you've ever tasted. I could have eaten it by the pan. It could absorb any flavor, so if you put, like, a single raspberry in it, the whole thing would be raspberry flavored."

"Not like the corn bread we had at dinner."

"Nah. Not like that at all," he said, really sad.

I sat up in bed. "Is that why you haven't been eating much? Was food there that different?"

Aidan sighed. "It was better. Everything tasted better. The tastes we have here seem faded now. Watered down. In Aveinieu it was so intense. I learned how to cook! You wouldn't believe it, Lucas. Some of the things I made . . . I know I wasn't there long, but it's like each meal was its own movie and symphony and light show all at once. That kind of intense."

"Sounds awesome."

"It was."

"You could try cooking here?"

"Nah. I can't do any of the things I did there. Not here. I can't explain it—I wasn't a different person, really. But the person I was meant something different. I had a different role."

I tried to picture him there. On a farm. Making magical corn bread. But my imagination couldn't reach it.

"What did you wear there?" I asked, figuring maybe more details would make it feel more real.

"Cordelia's friend Wei was this incredible seamstress.

She made me a shirt and some pants. It was almost like pajamas, but no elastic, just a drawstring. And the whole underpants thing was not something they did. So I kept washing mine in the river so I could rewear them."

"But when you came back, you were in your old pajamas."

"Yeah. I was sleeping in them when . . . well, when I was sent back."

"What happened?"

"Cordelia didn't think it was safe for me there anymore. I didn't agree. I thought she was making it up so I would go back. But in the end . . . she won."

"Why didn't she think it was safe for you?"

"I'm telling you—that was probably a lie. She said some of the creatures were worried I was bringing a plague with me. But honestly, I think she always regretted staying in Aveinieu. She missed her family. And since she couldn't go back, she made me go back."

"Why couldn't she go back?"

"Because when I told her what year it was, she realized everyone she'd ever known would already be dead."

"When did she leave here?"

"Over a hundred years ago."

"So she must've been really old."

"Not really. I told you, time moves differently there. Or maybe our bodies just age differently."

Are you making this up? I wanted to ask. *Are you lying to me the same way you lied to Glenn?* Some of the things he was telling me were possibly too convenient—starting with the fact that the food he mentioned was a variation of what we'd just eaten. But he also didn't seem to be stopping to think about his answers, and he hadn't contradicted himself yet.

So either he was a really good liar . . . or this wasn't a lie.

"Why'd they think you had a plague? Were you sick?" I asked.

"No. But the last person from our world had a form of measles—or at least that's what Cordelia thought it was. So of course the Aveinieu started to worry that all of us newcomers had it, and that it would spread. Which wasn't true. But it gave them a reason to be suspicious."

"Who's 'them'?"

"Some other humans. But mostly the animals. The maddoxes, the unicorns, the boarses."

"Boarses?"

"Kind of like a boar, kind of like a horse."

"And the birds? What did the birds think of you?"

There was a pause. Then Aidan said, "It was really strange—there weren't any birds. Cordelia said she wasn't sure whether it was true of all of Aveinieu or just the part we were in. Like, if it was two hundred years ago and you walked up to someone here and showed them a picture of a panda bear and asked them if they'd ever seen one, they would think it was a magical creature, right? They'd have no idea they existed half a world away. So maybe it was like that with birds. Although Cordelia said she'd never heard an Aveinieu story that included a bird. And there were a lot of Aveinieu stories. Cordelia said she only knew about one percent of one percent of one percent of all of them. That's how she put it."

I was going to ask more about Cordelia, but Dad's voice interrupted from the hall. "Guys, it's late. Time for bed."

"Sorry!" I called.

Aidan remained quiet until we heard Dad's footsteps trudge back to his room and our parents' bedroom door close.

"Do you think he heard?" Aidan asked.

"I don't think so," I said, because that was the answer he wanted.

"I hope not," he said. And I didn't ask, *Why not, if it's the truth?*

"Let's go to sleep," he said.

I wondered if he dreamed of Aveinieu, or if his dreams were as stuck here as he was.

25

Aunt Brandi arrived just before lunch on Sunday, and she brought along what felt like a year's supply of cinnamon rolls.

"If this doesn't cheer you up, I don't know what will," she said.

"You're a saint," Mom replied, taking the boxes and putting five cinnamon rolls out on a plate.

Growing up, Aunt Brandi had been Mom's little brother. But she had already begun living as her true female self by the time Aidan and I were born. She was always our favorite of our aunts and uncles . . . but the competition wasn't very serious. The rest of our aunts and uncles lived far away. And none of them would have brought cinnamon rolls.

We sat down at the table and ate. Mom used a fork and knife. Dad and Aidan ate their rolls section by section, unraveling the spirals as they went. I noticed that Aidan wasn't as hesitant as he'd been with the corn bread; maybe cinnamon rolls came close to the "intensity" of the Aveinieu cuisine.

Brandi and I just dug in, eating the middle in the middle. "So," Brandi said between bites, "how's everyone doing? I want to go around the table, starting with you, Laura."

"I'm enjoying this cinnamon roll very much," Mom said after putting down her fork and her knife.

Brandi *tsk*ed her sister. "You know that's not what I'm asking. How are you *doing*?"

"Obviously, I'm grateful that Aidan's home. And I'm exhausted from saying thank you to everyone who helped. And I'm feeling guilty for feeling so exhausted by that. And, of course, I'm frustrated that we don't know what really happened. But I am also at peace with that frustration because, as I said, the important thing is that we're all together again. Does that answer satisfy you, Brandi?"

Brandi nodded. "Absolutely. Your turn, Jim."

"Also grateful to be here like this," Dad said. "Because for a moment there it looked . . . Oh God. Sorry, guys." Dad's eyes had started to tear up, and now he was wiping it away.

"It's okay, Jim," Brandi said. Mom patted his back.

Dad took a deep breath, laughed a little at himself.

"Sorry again. Don't know what got into me. I guess it wasn't that long ago that Laura and I were sitting at this table with the police, them telling us . . ." Dad took another deep breath. "Them saying we couldn't give up hope, but the fact that they were saying that . . . it just felt like *they* were starting to lose hope. And we had to stare into that abyss and hope that somewhere in there, Aidan would take shape. Which he did. It's all good again."

Brandi was getting a little teary too. When I snuck a look at Aidan, he looked something between embarrassed and horrified.

"Your turn, Lucas," Brandi said.

"Glad to have Aidan back, duh."

"What else?"

"I don't know. I wish I had one of those devices from *Men in Black* that can erase everyone's memories. I'd love everyone to forget the past week, so we could really be back to normal instead of this *normal but* we're now in."

"What do you mean, *normal but?*"

I thought it was obvious. But I reminded myself that Aunt Brandi wasn't living with us, so she wouldn't necessarily know.

"Normal but everyone's looking at us funny," I explained. "Normal but there are all these questions that nobody's asking, but you can tell they really, really want to ask them. Normal but we were kinda on the news last week, and that doesn't disappear when you change the channel. Normal that we're a family again, but . . . we also have to deal with this big thing that happened to us."

"That makes perfect sense to me," Brandi said.

"Me too," Dad added, reaching over and messing my hair. "We'd all like to get rid of that pesky *but*."

Normally, Aidan would be all over Dad using the phrase "pesky but"—I half suspected Dad had said it just so Aidan could laugh at its resemblance to *pesky butt*. But Aidan didn't say a word.

At least not until Brandi turned to ask how he was doing. Before she could get a sentence out, *he* asked *her,* "So how are *you* doing?"

"Happy to be here, honestly," Brandi replied. "Things like this make you realize where you need to be. And I haven't been around enough."

"Oh, come on," Mom said. "You're here *plenty.*"

Brandi laughed, so I figured Mom was teasing. Or Brandi just refused to be offended by the accusation that she was around too much.

"Can I be excused?" Aidan asked.

This made Brandi laugh even louder. Then she sucked some dried frosting off her fingers and said, "No way, dude. It's your turn. So tell your auntie what's going on in that bright head of yours."

"There's no way for you to understand."

"Tell me."

"First, you tell me . . . do you think I'm lying, like my parents do?"

"We don't think you're lying," Dad jumped in and said.

Mom shushed him. "Let Brandi answer, Jim."

Aunt Brandi pushed her chair back and scooted it so she was facing Aidan directly. He turned her way.

"I'm going to be honest with you, kid, because I don't know any other way to be. I don't think you're lying on purpose. I think you absolutely believe what you're saying. And I respect that. Completely. But do I believe it's true? Again, if I'm being honest, the answer is: I have no idea. It stretches credibility—but life stretches credibility all the time, to the point that credibility doesn't have much credibility left, you know? What concerns me is that a lot of the time when we believe a story that's fantastic, it's in order to cover over something really traumatic that's happened. I am worried that someone hurt you, or that you hurt yourself, and that if the hurt isn't addressed, it's only going to get worse. I've tried to bury things, Aidan, and I can tell you—it doesn't work. Burying something doesn't take away the weight of it. It only pushes the weight deeper and makes it harder to carry around."

Aunt Brandi stopped and reached over to turn Aidan's chin so he was facing her perfectly.

"Do you hear me?" she asked.

He nodded.

"Good. Now . . . it's your turn. How are you doing?"

"I'm sad."

"And why are you sad?"

"Because I'm here."

"Do you mean in the kitchen right now, forced to have this conversation? Or do you mean *here* as opposed to *there*."

Aidan looked away from her, down to his lap. "I mean here as opposed to there."

"That's an awful thing to say!" Mom exclaimed at the same time Dad said, "Aw, Aidan, no."

Brandi ignored them. "That's hard, Aidan."

When he looked back up this time, he was angry.

"*I know that,*" he said, standing up. "None of you know! None of you were there! It's better, the way they do things—and it makes you realize how awfully we do things here, okay? They know how to get along with each other. And let people do their own thing. Not like here. None of you have *any idea.*"

He ran out of the room then. I thought he'd go to our room, but the footsteps kept going, up to the attic.

Mom and Dad both stood up.

"No," Aunt Brandi said. "Let him be alone for a little bit."

"Brandi," Mom said coolly, "that's not your call." She dropped her napkin on the table and headed upstairs, Dad following.

"Well, that went well!" Brandi said to me. "Want another cinnamon roll?"

I shook my head.

"Nah, me neither." She gave me a look similar to the one she'd just given Aidan, all this intense concentration. "Has he been talking to you?"

"A little," I said. "At night."

"That's good. And how does he seem to you?"

I thought about how all the fun of life seemed to have drained away from him, how the brother I knew who was so boisterous and out in the open was now stuck in his own head . . . or maybe stuck in a place that could only exist in his head right now.

"He seems lost," I told Brandi.

She sighed and sat back a little in her chair. "That makes sense. Whatever happened, it can't be easy to come back. It's like he needs what the astronauts had—two weeks in quarantine to settle back into our world and into their own heads after the adrenaline wore off. A decompression chamber. There's a lot of compression going on here, I'm sure."

"I'm not sure what you mean," I told her. "If we're being honest."

She laughed. "I guess what I'm saying is that whatever happened to Aidan, he went through it alone. And he's going to have to adjust to the idea that he's not alone anymore."

"I don't think he was alone there. In Aveinieu. It wasn't like that."

"Really?"

"Yeah, there was this woman he lived with, Cordelia. And there were other people too. And animals. Only they weren't like our animals."

And just like that, I found myself saying too much. I hadn't meant for what Aidan said to me at night to leave our room. Mostly because I knew that if he found out I'd blabbed, he wouldn't tell me anything else.

"You can't let anyone know I said that!" I quickly told Brandi. "If you want him to keep talking to me. And I'm the only one he's talking to!"

"It's okay, Lucas. Really, it's okay. Your secret is safe with me." She crossed her heart, then for good measure locked her mouth with an invisible key and threw the key my way. I caught it and put it in my pocket.

"Thanks," I said.

"No—thank *you*, for being there for him. As I told you before, he needs you in his corner."

As if to emphasize this, Mom and Dad came storming back into the kitchen, Dad in the lead this time, Mom following.

"You shouldn't have said that!" Mom was yelling at Dad. "Did you see how he reacted? It was like you were a monster."

"All I said was that if that stupid dresser was the problem, then the obvious solution was to get rid of it! I wasn't actually throwing it to the curb at that very moment!"

"Well, you might as well have! We all know the last thing we should do right now is make him more upset. But you just managed to do that beautifully. With an assist from my sister!"

"Whoa!" Brandi said. "How did this get to be my fault?"

"It's nobody's fault," Dad said. "Nobody's. Not mine. Not yours. Not Laura's. Not Aidan's. *Nobody's.*"

"Well, it's not the dresser's fault either!" Mom added. Dad didn't seem to appreciate this.

I wasn't really a part of the conversation, so I left. I went up to the attic and found Aidan sitting on the floor, facing the dresser. Its doors were closed.

"I know it isn't going to work again," Aidan said to me. "I know they cut the connection. But I still want it here. Just in case."

"Makes sense," I said, sitting down next to him.

We sat there in silence for about three minutes.

It was getting pretty boring. At least for me.

"Look," I said, "do you want to go see a movie? Let's make them take us to a movie."

"Alright," Aidan said. Then he stood up and left the room without looking back.

26

Although she wouldn't say it, I think Mom was glad to get the rest of us out of the house. She said she still had a lot of phone calls to make and thank-you cards to write. I tried to imagine what the cards said: *Thank you for trying to find my son, even though it ended up he was nowhere you could've reached. Next time we'll have to send you inside the furniture to get him!*

We went to our usual movie theater, downtown. Dad had gone there when he was a kid, and my grandmother had gone there when *she* was a kid. Our family and the movie theater had been in town a long time, and knew each other well.

Still, we weren't prepared for the reaction we got when we showed up. Louie, the owner, came out of the ticket office and exclaimed, "Here they are!" like we were the stars of the movie we were seeing. He gave Dad and Aidan bearish hugs.

"We looked everywhere for you!" he said to Aidan while Aidan was still enfolded in his arms. "Everywhere!"

"I'm sorry?" Aidan said with an actual smile.

Louie laughed and released him. "Don't be ridiculous. It's a hero's return! Whatever movie you're seeing, it's on me!"

Dad smiled and took out his wallet. "You don't have to do that, Louie. We're grateful for your help."

"No, no, no!" Louie exclaimed, waving Dad's wallet away. "I won't hear of it."

"Really," Dad said. "I insist."

I could see why Dad was uncomfortable. *I* was uncomfortable. Why should we be rewarded for Aidan disappearing on us?

Louie didn't see it this way, though. He saw it as something to celebrate, and eventually Dad gave in. Though once we were inside, he slipped Brandi some money and she went and bought tickets from the person at the window while Louie was busy with the popcorn.

So I guess nobody won.

As more and more people came into the theater, Aidan ducked lower and lower. It was only when the lights went down and the previews came on that he looked a little comfortable. But not as comfortable as *before*.

I wondered if we'd ever be as comfortable as *before*.

When we got home, Mom was already starting on dinner. ("An early dinner so Brandi can make an early start," she explained.)

Mom must have said something to Brandi while they set the table, because after that, Brandi didn't ask any more questions about Aidan's disappearance. Instead, we talked about the movie and about Brandi's projects at work and about wayward cousins of Mom's and Brandi's that I barely knew. When the phone rang, we didn't think much of it—the house phone had rung more in the past week than it had for probably the previous five years combined.

Mom looked at the caller ID and said, "Oh, it's Denise. I'll just tell her I'll call back."

Denise was Glenn's mom.

Mom picked up the phone. "Hi, Denise—we're in the middle of dinner. Can I call you back? . . . Oh, okay. What's going on? . . . I see. . . ." Mom leaned against the counter like she needed its support. "And who told you this? . . . And she heard it from? . . . Okay. I see. . . . Well, of course it isn't true, Denise. How could it be true? . . . I know. We all react in different ways, right? . . . Of course. . . . Absolutely. I appreciate you telling me. . . . Thank you, Denise. I'll call them right away. And I'll call you back later, okay?"

We had all stopped eating and were looking at her.

After she hung up the phone, she stared at it for a second, then put it back in its cradle.

"So," she said, coming back to the table without sitting down, "according to Denise, some people in town have apparently found out about Aidan's story. It was right there in the police report, and someone there saw it and couldn't help but share it with someone else, who probably told a few more people . . . and one of those people called Denise and asked her if it's true, if Aidan is really saying he was where he said he was. She told this person she had no idea what she was talking about. I, obviously, couldn't say the same."

Dad cursed out loud. Brandi shook her head and said something about small towns. Aidan looked like he wanted to fall through the floor.

"The whole town must know by now," Mom said. "Denise is the only one who had the decency to call me."

Aidan reached into his pocket and turned on his phone, which he'd shut off for the movie. It vibrated with missed messages. I looked over at the screen and saw most of them were from Glenn.

"I think we need a family meeting," Dad said.

"Jim, we're all at the table. You don't have to call it a meeting," Mom snapped. "Unless you're planning to take minutes?"

"C'mon, guys," Brandi said. "We're all on the same team here."

The phone rang again. Mom looked at the caller ID and didn't pick up.

"He's a minor," Mom said. "His statement shouldn't be left around for other people to read."

"True," Dad said. "But it doesn't really matter whether the story should have come out or not. What matters is that it's out there, and we have to figure out what to say."

"It's true," Aidan said. "The story."

It was as if two more bricks fell out of Dad's patience then, making it dangerously close to collapsing.

"Aidan," he said, voice barely under control, "you need to listen carefully now. We're not talking about whether or not it actually happened, whether or not you went into this other world. What we're talking about is everyone else knowing. Believe me when I say that you do *not* want to be known as the kid who said he went to a far-off kingdom while everyone here was killing themselves to try to find him. That will not go over well, and will follow you for the rest of your life."

"It's not a kingdom," Aidan said.

"What?" Dad shouted, exasperated.

"I think he's saying there wasn't any king," Brandi explained. "Therefore, not a kingdom."

"How is that helpful?" Mom asked.

"It's helpful," Brandi said carefully, "because Aidan needs our support right now, not our doubt."

"You do see how this looks, don't you?" Mom shot back. "You don't think we're being unreasonable to show concern about how it looks for Aidan, do you?"

Brandi kept her voice calm. "I absolutely understand that, Laura. The only way I can see for you to deal with it is to dismiss it, to say that Aidan was shaken up when he returned and invented a story to get the adults to leave him alone. I know you have to say that outside this house. But inside this house is something else. Inside this house, you need to listen to Aidan."

Aidan jumped in. "What can I do to prove it to you?" he asked our parents. "I can tell you all about it, if you want. I can draw you pictures. I can tell you the things I saw there that I never would see here. Just tell me what you want to know."

"We want to know what really happened, Aidan," Dad said. "That's all."

"The days were longer than twenty-four hours, and the way it worked was that you'd get up when the sun rose and go to sleep when the sun set, and that would still be enough time to get everything done and get enough sleep. The thing I slept on was more like a rug than a bed, but it was super comfortable. Every morning I'd roll it up and put it in the corner. And you know how they say breakfast is the most important meal of the day? Well, over there, they actually believe it. You spend the first hour of the day getting the meal ready and making your plans for the day. There isn't any coffee there, just tea. And the tea isn't in bags or anything. There's this flower they called a plenty, and you'd put the roots of the plenty into the hot water for one flavor or you'd put the petal side into the hot water for another flavor. I liked the petal side more, though the root side was supposed to keep you awake. And there were animals there, all these kinds of animals. Like boarses, that were part boar and part horse, and maddoxes, that were like wolves mixed with oxen."

Aidan seemed happier the more he was telling us these things, as his mind went back and remembered.

Mom and Dad didn't seem happier. They looked concerned. Like Aidan had really lost his mind.

I imagined I looked a lot like Brandi looked—part amazed by what Aidan was saying and part amazed by the fact that he was talking to us at all. And underneath the amazement, there was a tiny question: Weren't maddoxes supposed to be bears mixed with oxen, not wolves? Wasn't that what he'd told me? Did it really matter?

The phone rang again. This time when Mom saw the caller ID, she picked up.

"Hello, Officer Pinkus. . . . Yes, we have definitely heard what's being said. I hope you are calling to tell us how to make it go away, because other than that, I'd say your department has done enough harm to my son for one night."

None of the rest of us could hear what Officer Pinkus said in response to that, but it must have done something to make Mom a little less angry, because as the conversation continued, her tone was a little less harsh. Dad and Brandi didn't even try to distract me and Aidan from listening; we were all silent at the table, waiting for Mom to finish.

"Well," Mom said when the call was through, "it sounds like they're trying to do some damage control." She sat down at the table. "There was a reporter who called, and the police told them there wasn't a story. And apparently the chief dressed down the person who leaked the report in the first place. Officer Pinkus thinks it'll pass. She suggested we ignore it, and if anyone asks, we can say the police have told us not to reveal where Aidan really was. She felt comfortable with that. Although of course, Aidan, she's hoping that when she comes by tomorrow night, after school and after your appointment with Dr. Jennings, you'll have more to tell her."

"I'm not going to school tomorrow," Aidan said.

Mom didn't blink. "Of course you are. Why wouldn't you?"

"Because the whole school is going to treat me like I'm weird?"

"Just tell them it isn't true," Dad advised. "Laugh at it before they start laughing at you."

I thought Aidan was going to fight it further. It was more disturbing when he instantly gave up. He didn't say anything else, just ate his dinner until there wasn't anything left on his plate.

The phone rang again. And again.

Mom waited until we were out of the kitchen to start calling people back.

Aidan sequestered himself in the den again with the TV. I stayed in our room. When I heard footsteps in the attic, I couldn't ignore them. I went upstairs and found Aunt Brandi standing in front of the dresser.

"I just had to see it," she said when I walked up next to her. "It's so . . . ordinary. You know, there are things in this attic that belonged to my grandparents—that chest over there was actually my great-grandparents', which would make them your great-great-grandparents. It's traveled the world, been through wars. And that dusty lime-green couch in that corner, under all that stuff? That was from your parents' first apartment. Your mother would *never* dream of sitting on something so dusty, but she's never going to get rid of it, because it was one of the first things that was theirs together." She turned back to Aidan's dresser. "But this thing? It has no history. Your mom bought it in a store. There are probably thousands out there just like it."

"Do you think they all lead to Aveinieu?" I asked.

Aunt Brandi hiccupped a laugh. "I doubt it. If that were true, I imagine we would have heard a lot more about Aveinieu by now."

"So how does it work?"

"I don't know. I don't even know if there's a way for us to know. There's definitely no way for Aidan to know. If what he says happened really happened, it's far beyond our science and our language. If we're lucky, we can know the *what*. But the *how* and the *why*? This dresser has about as much of a chance of explaining that to us as Aidan does."

"Aidan keeps saying we can't understand."

"He's right. But that doesn't mean *he* understands it. None of us can understand it. Some people will accept that. Other people won't. They get scared by things they don't understand. Those are the people to be careful around. But they don't get to dictate our reality."

Aunt Brandi took a deep breath and sighed it out. Then she touched the side of the dresser as if she was touching the shoulder of an old friend.

"I told your parents I could stay, help out. Call in sick from work for a few days, or work from here. But they don't see any reason for me to be here. They think they can handle it on their own. I think they're wrong, but I respect that I don't get a vote. Still, they can't stop me from telling you to call me—anytime, any hour. I will drop anything to come back here for you and Aidan. Because you know what, Lucas?"

"What?" I asked.

Aunt Brandi sighed again. "There's nothing we can do about it . . . but I guarantee you, tomorrow's really going to suck."

27

"It might only be a few parents who've heard," Mom said as we pulled into the school driveway the next morning. "I doubt any of the kids will know. I mean, why would the parents tell their kids?"

Dad stayed quiet.

For a brief moment when we got into school, I thought Mom might have actually been right. A lot of kids were looking at us, but they weren't laughing at us. It was almost like Friday all over again. People were curious . . . but that was about it.

Or at least that's what I thought until I started to see the whispering. One kid telling another kid something, and then both of them looking in our direction in a way that was much less curious and much more judgmental.

"Dude!" Glenn called out as soon as he saw us come in. "What's going on?"

"Hey!" Aidan said, stretching to reach a carefree, off-hand tone—in other words, stretching to sound like himself. "Sorry I couldn't text you back last night. Things were totally bonkers."

"I figured. I know my mom talked to your mom—can you believe that crazy story going around? I mean, what's up with that?"

Glenn wasn't being quiet with his question. I felt like the whole hallway had heard it.

Aidan tried to keep the same hey-dude tone he usually used with Glenn when he said, "I have *no idea* what's up with that."

Glenn laughed. "I mean, right? *Unicorns?* Why in the world would the police think you said you were off with *unicorns?*"

I wanted to interrupt. I wanted to ask, *Why are you asking him this in public? Why can't you wait?*

"Look, dude," Aidan said. "Do you want to hear the truth?"

"Totally," Glenn replied.

Aidan took a deep breath. We were at his locker now, so we all stopped. Only a few of the balloons from Friday were still there, and they'd shrunk over the weekend. The streamers didn't stream as bright. Usually I would have kept walking to my own locker—but not now. I wanted to hear what Aidan had to say, in no small part because I was sure I'd be quizzed about it later by other people, including our parents.

"Okay," Aidan said, "it's like this: You know how I told you I didn't have much to eat when I was away, and how I was sick and everything? Well, by the time I got back to my house, I was a little out of my mind. Or maybe a lot out of my mind. It's amazing I found my way home at all. And once I did . . . the police asked me where I'd been, and I just told them this thing that was more like a dream than reality. I mean, unicorns and green skies and everything. It wasn't until I caught up on my sleep and got some food that I started to make any kind of sense. It's, like, so stupid that the police wrote down what I was saying, and it's even stupider that other people heard about it."

"Oh, man," Glenn said, shaking his hand. "You're right. It's *so* stupid."

Aidan surprised me then by turning to me and asking, "Didn't I seem out of my mind that night?"

No, I thought. *You seemed to know exactly what you were saying.*

"Yeah," I said. "Completely out of your mind."

"They said you were found in the attic?" Glenn said.

"Yup," Aidan said, opening his locker. "I have no memory of how I got there."

"That's so unreal!"

"I know, right?" Aidan got out his books, then swung the locker shut. More balloons fell off. "Look," he said to Glenn, "you have to keep what I told you between us. I mean, you can tell people that I wasn't thinking straight when I told the police about the unicorns and everything. But the part about where I really went—that's gotta be secret. The police are still trying to figure it out, and I just . . . well, I just don't want everyone else to know, okay? You're my best friend, so I don't mind you knowing. But not everyone else. I just want life to be what it was, right?"

"Totally, totally," Glenn said. "Your secret is safe with me. Nobody else needs to know."

"Cool," Aidan said. "Now tell me what you got up to yesterday."

They started to walk to Glenn's locker; since mine was in the other direction, I said "See ya" to them both. Aidan gave me a "Yeah, see ya" back. Glenn kept walking.

Busby found me a few steps before I got to my locker. She was breathless from running to get there.

"I just heard from Caleb who heard from Nick who said his dad heard from another dad that Aidan said he was sucked into another dimension while we were looking for him here—is that true?!?"

"Um, yes," I said. "I mean, no. I mean, yes."

If Busby was my test on whether I could pull off lying for Aidan, I was failing big-time. I decided to try again before she said anything else.

"I mean, the answer is yes, Aidan did say that, but no, he didn't actually go into another world. It was a big mix-up. A total misunderstanding."

"Oh," Busby said, catching her breath. "That's disappointing."

"It is?"

"Yeah. It would have been much more fun if he'd actually met some unicorns."

I couldn't help but remember that I'd been the one to chime in about unicorns that night. If only I'd known it was the one thing about Aveinieu that would stick in people's minds, I would have kept my mouth shut.

It became pretty easy for me to tell the people who'd heard from the people who hadn't heard yet. Teachers didn't seem to have heard anything. If they treated me any different from before Aidan's disappearance, it was still with concern about how my family and I were doing.

Students for the most part were sticking to Principal Kahler's rule about not asking too many questions. Some kids acted like they'd already forgotten. But some—the ones, I assumed, who'd heard about the unicorns—were still giggling their way through the whisper network, looking at me with minimally disguised smiles. And if I was getting that, I could only imagine the way Aidan was being treated.

Glenn must have been sharing Aidan's out-of-his-mind excuse, because by lunchtime, it felt like there were two whisper networks competing with each other. One was saying that Aidan was crazy because he thought he'd gone to a fantasy world. Another was saying Aidan had only been temporarily crazy, long enough to make up a fantasy story. Nobody was calling him a liar—not yet. Instead they were focused on when, exactly, he'd lost his mind.

I got updates about this from Busby, Tate, and Truman. They thought they were doing me a favor by telling me what everyone was saying . . . and who knows? Maybe they *were* doing me a favor. It probably would have been worse if I hadn't known what was being said. But at the same time, it was frustrating, because there was no way for me to correct it. Once a story was out there, it could be turned into any other story a person wanted to tell. It was no longer Aidan's, but Aidan was still getting all the attention for it.

I didn't see him until pickup time at the end of the day. His locker no longer had any balloons or streamers on it. I didn't know if he'd pulled them down or if someone else had. I didn't want to ask.

I got there as he was bent over his book bag, so I couldn't really see his face. Before I could ask him how his day was, Glenn came up behind me, saying, "Oh, man, that was so uncool. I hope you know that. It was *so* uncool."

Aidan stood up straight, saw me, then looked at Glenn.

"It *was* uncool," he said. "But no worries. I mean, whatever."

"What happened?" I asked.

"Seriously," Glenn said, as if I hadn't opened my mouth. "Keegan needs to chill out. Especially, like, in front of everyone else. I can't believe he did that."

"Did what?" I asked.

"It's fine," Aidan said. "I'm fine. People are going to be jerks about it—I get that. Hopefully they'll move on to being jerks about something else soon."

"Will someone please tell me what's going on?" I said. It sounded more like a whine than I wanted it to.

"It's nothing," Aidan said dismissively.

Strangely, it was Glenn who decided to fill me in.

"We had a sub in English," he said, "which meant it basically turned into an out-of-control study hall. Keegan Ronson thought he was real funny, so he went to the closet in the classroom, poked his head in, then shouted, 'Hey, Aidan—there's a unicorn in here who wants to talk to you!' And once he got a laugh, he poked his head back in, then came out and said something like, 'Yeah, and there's a dragon here who says she's your girlfriend and you really need to reply to her texts.' Which got a bigger laugh, even though most kids in class had no idea what he was talking about, and the substitute really didn't know what he was talking about, but assumed it was, like, a reference to what we were reading in class. Which was kinda funny, since we're reading *Walk Two Moons.* Which doesn't, you know, have any dragons or unicorns in it."

"I really don't care," Aidan said, closing his locker and heading for the exit.

"Yeah," Glenn went on. "People are really stupid. Kelli McGillis, who's always flirt-fighting with Keegan, was like, 'I don't think Aidan's here—I think he attends Hogwarts now.' And, like, a few kids laughed at that, but at that point a bunch of us were just like, hey, it's time for everyone to shut up now. It was so uncool."

Aidan was now ahead of us, out of the conversation.

"How did Aidan respond?" I asked Glenn.

"I thought he was going to joke right back at them, but he just kinda took it, you know? Didn't laugh, but didn't try to fight it either. It was like he was pretending none of it was happening. Which was cool, because there wasn't more fuel for the fire, and with people like Keegan and Kelli, they tend to die out when there's no more fuel."

I wanted to ask Glenn if he thought it really had died out, or whether people were going to keep making stupid, uncool comments. But we were out the door now and at the curb, where both my mom and dad were waiting, this time in separate cars. Aidan went into Mom's car without saying bye to me or Glenn; she was taking him to the therapist's office. I said bye to Glenn, who grunted a goodbye to me in response. Then I got into Dad's car.

"Right on time," he said as I put on my seat belt and he pulled away from the school. "How'd it go today?"

"We made it through," I replied.

"That bad, huh?" he asked, looking at me all concerned.

"No, it was fine," I said.

"Were kids mean to Aidan?"

"You'd have to ask Aidan."

"Well, how about you?"

"Everyone was fine with me. Totally fine."

"Did your friends hear about what Aidan said?"

"Yup. A lot of people mentioned unicorns."

"That doesn't sound good."

"No, but I think it could have been worse. It's a joke— that's all. People think it's weird or funny. Aidan told Glenn that he was in a daze or something when he said it. Glenn seemed to believe that."

Dad took that in for a moment and then said, "That's interesting. Aidan didn't insist it was true?"

"He's not dumb, Dad. He knows that no one's going to believe he was missing in a make-believe world."

"And which story do you believe?"

It didn't seem fair for him to be asking me this. But still I gave Dad the most honest answer I could think of, which was: "I think it's complicated."

He nodded. "That it is."

"What do *you* believe?" I asked.

Dad hesitated for a moment, then said, "I don't believe in fantasy worlds, Lucas. I just don't. Or can't. So I guess that means I don't believe what Aidan is saying about Aveinieu. But unlike a lot of people, including your mother, at the end of the day I don't really care where Aidan was for those six days, as long as he wasn't hurt and no one else is being hurt. If Aidan was hiding somewhere else the whole time, then felt he needed to come up with an incredible story in order to justify what he put us through . . . I'm genuinely okay with that. We all make mistakes, and I suspect Aidan made a big one. Even though we were all so scared, nobody was hurt. Life goes on. And I'm hoping that Aidan's life will go on too, and eventually it won't matter to anyone where he was. We'll forget it ever happened."

"I don't care either," I said.

"Good." Dad looked at me. "But, Lucas? If he does tell

you something about where he was, you need to tell us, okay? We'll never let him know you told us. We just need to make sure something like this doesn't happen again."

I didn't want to spy on Aidan for my parents. But at the same time, I knew if I told my father I wasn't going to do it, he'd think I already knew something and wasn't telling.

Dad went on. "I keep wondering if Aveinieu is from a book or a movie or a game. It's not like Aidan to make up fantasy worlds in his head. It's not like he reads that many fantasy novels, right?"

"Right," I said. Aidan pretty much only read books set during World War II.

"He had to have gotten the story from somewhere. It's not the kind he'd invent all by himself."

Doesn't that make it more believable? I wanted to ask. But I knew better than to say that.

When we got home, I went to Aidan's bookshelf, to make sure I was right about what he read. There wasn't any C. S. Lewis or Garth Nix or Holly Black. There was a lot of Alan Gratz and Deborah Hopkinson instead. I took out each of the books I didn't know and read the back covers, to see if any resembled the stories Aidan had told me about Aveinieu. I searched for green skies and unicorns, boarses and maddoxes. I couldn't find a single one.

Eventually I put all the books back on the shelf and started my homework. I was on the floor surrounded by textbooks when Aidan returned from his appointment with the psychiatrist.

"How'd it go?" I asked, looking up from my math book.

Aidan dropped his book bag on the floor and headed for his bed. "It was okay, I guess."

"What did you say?"

"I told him I didn't want to talk about what happened. And he said that was fine, if I didn't mind him asking questions about before. I said I was okay with that, so he asked me all about Mom and Dad, and about sharing a room with you, and about whether I ever felt the need to run away."

"What did you answer?"

"I told him the truth: I've never had any desire to run away. I tried once or twice when I was little, I think, but that was just for attention, and I didn't really mean it. I told him I was happy here."

"But you would've stayed there?"

"What?"

"What you said the other night, that you wished you hadn't had to leave Aveinieu. If you're happy here, why would you want to stay there?"

Aidan leaned forward, clutching a pillow in his lap. "Because it was incredible! Because I was doing something nobody else had ever gotten a chance to do, not like that. I felt . . ."

"Different?" I offered.

"No. Important. I felt important. I was making a hundred new discoveries every day."

"But you can discover things here too."

"Yeah, but they're things a lot of people have already discovered. If I discover something in a book, someone else had to know it already in order to write it down. If Mom or Dad tells me something, then they have to know it first. In Aveinieu, I was the first person from my part of the world to see everything. I was seeing things no book has ever been written about and no one else in my life has ever been through."

"Did you tell Dr. Jennings that?"

Aidan leaned back against the wall, crossing his legs on his bed. "No. He didn't ask. I told him, 'Look, I know everyone thinks something's wrong with me. But nothing's wrong with me. I'm back. I'll play along.'"

"Play along?"

"You know what I mean. If people don't want me to talk about Aveinieu, I'm fine with saying I was out of my mind, totally blabbering. I'd never planned to tell anyone. I was happier keeping it to myself."

I didn't know whether he was fishing for an apology from me for telling about Aveinieu in the first place . . . but I didn't think he was. It wasn't about that.

Aidan reached over to his bedstand to get his headphones. "Look, I just want to zone out for a while. The police are coming in an hour. I'm just going to lie down until then."

He moved to put his headphones on.

"Just one thing," I said, stopping him.

"What?"

"Remind me what maddoxes are again?"

"They're like . . . bears and oxen. Why? Do you think you saw one?"

That last question was like having the old Aidan back. So maybe that's why I didn't follow up with the natural question: *Why did you say maddoxes were something different last night?*

Instead, I made him think I was satisfied with his answer, and asked, "Do you want me to turn off the lights?"

"Nah," he said. "This is fine."

He left me then, as surely as if he'd walked out of the room. I was alone with my homework until Mom came up to tell us the detectives had arrived.

28

We weren't in the kitchen this time; we were in the den. Officer Ross wasn't there with Officer Pinkus; there was another officer, who introduced himself as Sergeant Jones. Mom and Dad seemed to know him already, but I hadn't seen him in the house during Aidan's disappearance. And obviously Aidan hadn't seen him, since he'd been . . . away.

"First off," Officer Pinkus said, "we want to apologize to you, Aidan, and to your whole family for the leak that came from our department. The person who told your story has been reprimanded—and I want to assure you that it was *not* someone who is working on your case anymore."

"We can accept your apology," Mom said, "as long as you can tell us how we get this back in its box. I cannot tell you how many calls I've gotten today. Wendy McGillis, in particular, has called me on my cell phone, at my office, and here at the house, asking for 'official comment.' That scares me. And the posts on the local message boards scare me even more."

"What posts in particular?" Office Pinkus asked.

"Please tell me you read the message boards," Mom answered. "If you want to know anything about this town, you go to the mommy message boards. And, frankly, they've turned against Aidan. They are angry that they were so inconvenienced when they had to search for his body last week. Back then, a whole week ago, they offered prayers and help. Now they only seem to have criticism and snark to offer."

Sergeant Jones scribbled something down on his pad. "We'll definitely check that out," he said.

"That's not enough," Mom insisted. "Not nearly enough. I want you to tell me how you're going to ensure my son's safety and prevent him from becoming the object of scorn and ridicule because one of your officers couldn't keep his mouth shut."

I couldn't believe Mom was talking to the police in the same voice she used to send me and Aidan to our room for misbehaving.

Officer Pinkus looked like she understood why she was in trouble, and accepted the punishment. "Look," she said, "there's no question mistakes were made. And I know you talked to Julia about how to deal with Ms. McGillis and any other members of the press. We didn't stop looking out for your family after Aidan returned. We are still looking out for you, and will help in any way we can. I suggest we discuss this more after Sergeant Jones and I ask Aidan our questions. As everyone in this room knows, this was meant to be a follow-up visit from last Thursday. I know a lot has happened since then, but we still have questions about Aidan's whereabouts last week. Aidan, do you mind if we ask you a few more questions?"

It wasn't like Aidan could say no, he'd rather not answer anything else about his disappearance ever again.

"Sure," he told the police.

"Okay," said Officer Pinkus, checking her notes. "Now that you've had more time to think about what happened, and hopefully you don't feel as on the spot as you might have on Thursday . . . is there anything you told us that you'd like to change? Or anything you'd like to add?"

Aidan had to have known the police would ask him this, but still he acted like he needed some time to think. Finally, he looked at Officer Pinkus and asked, "Do you want me to lie to you?"

"Aidan!" Mom said. But Officer Pinkus didn't seem to mind the question.

"Why are you asking me that?" she asked back.

"Because," Aidan said, "I've been lying to people all day. I told them that I was completely out of it when I talked to you on Thursday, and that I didn't know what I was saying. I told them my story was all made up, like I was really drunk on exhaustion and talking like a drunk person. I told them it was make-believe because there was no way to make them believe it. So if you want me to tell you the same things, I will. I'll tell you exactly what I said to them. But I also want you to know that I'll be lying to you. Because everything I said to you on Thursday was the actual truth."

When Aidan was done, I didn't watch him or the police officers. I watched our parents. Mom looked like she wanted to pull down the ceiling and scream. Dad looked like he wanted to fold himself into the couch and cry.

As for me—I was just trying to understand why Aidan hadn't decided to lie to them too.

Officer Pinkus didn't write anything down in her pad. She didn't break her eye contact with Aidan.

"I appreciate you sticking to the actual truth," she said. There was no judgment in her voice, no doubt. "That is, at the end of the day, the only thing I can ask of you is to give me the truth as you see it."

Sergeant Jones, I noticed, stayed silent.

"I have to tell you, Aidan," Officer Pinkus continued gently, "I spent the whole weekend checking our databases for something similar, some other mention of Aveinieu or another world described in the same way. It appears your case is unique. That isn't to say that it's wrong—it's only to say that it's singular."

134

"Probably because everyone else who's gone there has stayed," Aidan offered.

Officer Pinkus nodded. "That is absolutely a valid explanation. Which leads to my next question: Can you remember the names of the other people from our world who were there? Names and any details—the towns they came from, the dates they left. If you give me their names, I can put them into our database and see if they match any open missing persons cases."

It was hard to tell who was more surprised by this question: Mom and Dad, because it took what Aidan was saying so seriously, or Aidan, because it took what he was saying so seriously.

"I'm trying to think," he said. "Cordelia is the one I knew the most, but she never told me her last name. Just the initial, R. There weren't enough of us there to need last names. Ming was from China. There was a young woman named Heidi who spoke English. She said she was from Canada, and had been in Aveinieu for twenty years. But I don't know how that translates to our time. And I never asked her where in Canada. We never really talked about home. I was too busy trying to figure out Aveinieu."

"I just need one full name," Officer Pinkus said. "Preferably from the US, since I have more access here."

Aidan thought about it, then shook his head. "I don't know. We were isolated on the farm. Cordelia had a friend from New York named Joel. But I never met him. He'd left a few years before me. Joel P. Cordelia said he'd wanted to explore more of the world—but he never came back to tell her what he'd found."

"And Cordelia was from here? Did she tell you when she left?"

"A long time ago. That's all I know."

"You stayed with her the whole time?"

Aidan nodded.

"What did she look like?"

"She had this long red hair, with some gray in it. Her skin was tan—she liked to joke that she was lucky that she wasn't fair like her sister because she would have burned under the Aveinieu sun. It's not like there's sunscreen there."

"Did she make the joke about sunscreen?" Officer Pinkus asked.

"I don't think so. I did. Why?"

"It was a long shot. If she'd mentioned a particular kind of sunscreen, or sunscreen in general, we might have been able to pinpoint her age better."

It was the first time I'd realized there hadn't always been such a thing as sunscreen.

Officer Pinkus is pretty smart, I thought.

And then I thought, *But if she's so smart, why is she acting like she believes Aidan?*

It must be to make him talk, I concluded.

But Aidan only had so much to say. She asked him a few more times about other people, but he said he couldn't remember anything else. Then she asked him why he'd come back, and he explained to her why he'd been banished. That was the word he used: *banished.*

"It makes sense that there might be viruses or illnesses that we have in this world that they wouldn't necessarily have the immunity to in another world," Officer Pinkus said. "Isn't that right, Raymond?"

Sergeant Jones nodded. "Of course."

Officer Pinkus closed her notebook. "I think that's all I need right now," she said. Then, as if it was an afterthought, she added, "Oh—one more thing. Why the dresser?"

I could see Aidan waver slightly. "I don't know," he said. "I was surprised, and they never told me how it works. I asked, and Cordelia said she had no idea either. 'Our brains aren't big enough to comprehend the connections between worlds,' she said. She said my guess was as good as hers, and odds were strong that both guesses would be totally wrong."

Officer Pinkus smiled. "Cordelia sounds like my kind of person. It's lucky she was the first person you met, and not someone a lot less friendly."

"I know, right?" Aidan said. "I thought that a lot."

Mom and Dad exchanged a glance, like Cordelia was a neighbor they needed to go have a talk with.

"Okay, boys," Officer Pinkus said. "Time for me to chat with your parents. I'm going to trust you to not listen on the other side of the door, okay? I'll be back tomorrow to check in—and, Aidan, if you think of anything else, or anyone else who was there, be sure to write it down. And if it's something you feel is urgent to tell me, your parents have my number and you can call anytime, day or night."

"Thanks," Aidan said. And even if our parents didn't get the message, I did:

The way to get Aidan to appreciate you was to listen to what he had to say.

29

Officer Pinkus had asked us not to listen at the door. She hadn't said anything about listening from the staircase.

I pointed out this loophole to Aidan as we walked upstairs.

"Don't be stupid," he said. He went into our room, grabbed his laptop, and headed for the attic.

I definitely got the sense that I was not welcome to follow him.

So I stayed on the top stair and listened. I figured he'd be grateful later, if I found out something interesting to tell him.

I couldn't hear every word, but I could hear enough.

Cordelia's name came up a lot. Mom and Dad were asking if the police thought there was a "real Cordelia," as if the Cordelia from Aveinieu had a counterpart in our world.

At one point, Dad said, "Aidan was always the stable one," which made me wonder if I was the unstable one. That didn't sound right.

Mom brought up Wendy McGillis again. The moment she did, the phone rang. I was going to pick it up, but Dad yelled, "Don't pick up the phone!" I stayed put.

Then I heard a door opening. I worried that my parents had heard me breathing or something. So I backed off, toward my room.

"Don't pick up the phone if it rings!" Dad yelled again.

Soon I could hear the officers leaving. I decided I should tell Aidan it was okay to come down, so I went up to the attic.

I expected Aidan to be in front of the open dresser, studying it again. But instead he was on the old rocking chair our mom had used when we were babies and she wanted to rock us to sleep. He was working on his laptop and didn't tell me to go away when he saw me.

"I think it's over," I told him. "The police are heading home. Or back to the station. Or wherever it is they go after talking to us."

I was babbling, which Aidan would have never said was my best state. I then followed up with one of his least-favorite questions for me to ask: "What're you doing?"

"Just searching," he said.

I went and looked over his shoulder. He had *Aveinieu* typed into Google. There weren't any helpful results.

"How do you know how to spell it?" I asked.

"Cordelia told me. And someone must have told her. So I think if anyone else came back here, that's how they'd spell it. Though I'll try other spellings later."

"What if you're the only one?" I asked.

Aidan sighed. "Then no one will ever really believe me, I guess. I know I have to get used to that. But it would definitely make it better if there was someone else. Then I'd know for sure."

"For sure that you'd been there?"

"For sure that it really exists."

30

Aunt Brandi texted me for an update. I didn't know what to tell her.

The day sucked like you said it would, I started.

Then I added,

Aidan is sticking to his story.

She texted back, *What he says is what matters. What everyone else says is much less important.*

I wanted that to be true, but I wasn't sure. We had to live with everyone else. There was no way around that.

Mom and Dad decided to order pizza for dinner. Dad called it in. Then they both forgot, and when the doorbell rang, they jumped and panicked.

"Who could that be?" Mom asked. "It better not be Wendy McGillis."

"It's the pizza," I said. "Remember?"

Dad laughed. Mom didn't.

But I noticed that when Dad opened the door to get the pizza, he didn't open it all the way.

It was like he was afraid to let anyone see inside.

I was hoping to ask Aidan more questions—about maddoxes, about Cordelia, about anything he was willing to tell me. But when I got back to our room after brushing my teeth, he was already asleep. Or at least pretending to be.

The phone was ringing, and kept ringing all night.

I guess we got used to it enough to stay asleep.

31

"Boys. Wake up."

It was Mom's voice and it wasn't time to wake up yet. I looked at my clock. I was confused.

"What's going on?" Aidan asked, his voice still sleep-choked.

I rubbed my eyes, tried to focus on Mom and Dad standing in the middle of our room.

"Julia from the police department is downstairs with two officers," Mom explained. "She's going to help us. There's a television van outside, and a reporter who's setting up in the front yard. We are not answering the door or making any comment—Julia is going to handle all that for us. You two are going to have to stay home today, and you're going to need to listen to us very carefully. Under no circumstances are you to open the door or answer the phone or even look out the window. The shades are drawn and the doors are locked, and they need to stay that way. Julia says it's just the morning news, and the reporter should be gone within an hour. She also says we're lucky there's only one station here. That means the story isn't being picked up too widely."

"How did they find out?" Aidan asked.

Mom looked at Dad, as if he was the only one who had the answer.

"There was a story in the *News* this morning," he said. "Written by Wendy McGillis. I believe she's a mom at your school."

Aidan was sitting up now, his feet on the floor.

"Can I see it?" he asked.

Dad hesitated, but Mom nodded and he took out his phone. I sat down next to Aidan on his bed so I could see too.

It was from one of the city papers nearby, known for its big headlines and small amounts of truth.

THE BOY WHO CRIED UNICORN

Local town searched everywhere for missing boy.
Now he says he was off in another world.

They didn't name Aidan, but anyone who'd been paying attention last week would have remembered who he was. We'd been all over the news . . . and now the news was all over us. Some of the details from the police report were in the article, as well as a big "shame on you for reporting rumors about a minor" from Sergeant Jones and a few quotes from "local parents" who were glad Aidan was home but "distressed" that they had been "lied to" and "misled."

"We thought he might be dead," one parent was quoted in the last line of the article. "But he was probably just taking a vacation."

Nobody, it seemed, believed the vacation had actually taken place in Aveinieu. They thought Aidan had pulled a prank, and was making fun of them with his story.

"This isn't good," Aidan said when he was done reading.

"No, it isn't," Dad said, taking back his phone.

The doorbell rang. Once. Twice.

None of us moved.

It was only when there wasn't a third ring that Mom said, "You guys should go back to bed. Dad and I will be with the police downstairs. I'll call Denise and ask her to have Glenn pick up your homework."

Mom and Dad left, closing the door behind them.

"What channel is it?" Aidan asked me. Then, when I gave him my best *How am I supposed to know?* look, he gestured to the window and said, "Peek out from the side and see what channel it says on the van."

It was useless to tell him that was exactly what Mom

had just told us not to do. I went over to the window, pulled the shade out a little, and looked out.

"Channel Seven," I reported.

Aidan opened his laptop. "Okay. Got it."

I put the shade back and sat back beside him.

There was suddenly a buzzing in the room—both of our phones vibrating at once. Aidan reached for his and showed me it was a text from Brandi.

Those jerks, she wrote. *Don't they remember the whole point of the boy who cried wolf is that in the end he was TELLING THE TRUTH?*

The message was just for me and Aidan. My parents weren't on it.

Aidan texted her back a wolf emoji.

On his laptop, someone was doing the weather report in front of a map that made America look like it was tie-dyed. Then there were some commercials.

"At least you're not the biggest story," I said.

After the commercial, we were back in the news-room. The anchor mentioned our town, then, "Live with the story . . . Adam Goldman. What have you found out, Adam?"

"There are lots of questions swirling around this town," the reporter said from our front yard. "And they all come down to the fabulous story a twelve-year-old boy told. Last week, life came to a standstill for local residents as they desperately searched for him. Now they've learned that his alibi is something out of a fantasy novel."

"Only people accused of a crime need an alibi," I pointed out.

"Shhh," Aidan chided.

It was surreal to think that the reporter was maybe fifty feet away from us but we were still watching him on a screen. Then the story jumped to a nearby diner, where he'd interviewed "local people" about what had happened. I didn't recognize a single one of them.

"Kids today think they can say whatever they want," an older woman said, shaking her head. "I don't even blame the kids. It's the parents. They let them get away with everything."

An even older man sitting across from her said, "I figure that family owes the town the full cost of the search, if he was okay the whole time and now wants to lie about it."

The report returned to our front yard, focusing on our front door.

"The child's parents refused to comment," the reporter said. "According to police spokesperson Julia Koblish, the investigation is ongoing, and whatever the story he told when he returned, they're just happy this has ended up being much more a comedy than the tragedy it could have been."

"Thanks, Adam," the anchor said. "When you go to the acupuncturist, are you sure the needles are always clean? In her investigative report, Stacey Martinez goes undercover to see whether your pressure points are really safe. Stacey?"

Aidan closed the Channel 7 window and found the *News* story.

"That has to be Kelli McGillis's mom," he said when we were done reading the article again. "Figures."

There wasn't any way that we'd go back to sleep, so instead Aidan loaded up a two-player game and played me without complaint. When school started elsewhere, we began to get texts from our friends, all of them asking what was going on. I group-messaged Busby, Truman, and Tate and told them it was all a plot on my part to get out of school, mwahaha. Aidan was a little more serious with Glenn, telling him we were pretty much trapped inside, even though the camera crew was probably gone. (I pulled back the shade again; they were indeed gone.) Glenn asked for more of the scoop, to which Aidan replied, *What scoop? You know what happened.*

Glenn texted back: *Totally. Got it.*

Mom, Dad, and Julia from the police all checked up on us. Once the police were gone ("but still patrolling," Mom assured us), Dad made pancakes and tried to pretend it was a holiday or something, where we all had the day off. The phone kept ringing, and Mom always checked the caller ID before answering.

Dad told us that Julia had said the question would be whether Channel 7 or other stations would be back for the six o'clock news. "Hopefully someone in Washington will tweet something stupid and the attention will move somewhere else," Dad said.

It wasn't that I wanted to go to school, but it was strange to be stuck inside our house. Even when Aidan had been missing, it wasn't like we'd been confined indoors. The whole day, Mom and Dad kept the shades drawn, as if there might be reporters with telephoto lenses waiting for us to slip up. For all I knew, there *were* reporters with telephoto lenses outside.

I was reminded of the goldfish we'd had when I was in second grade. Just one goldfish in a simple bowl, it spent its day swimming around and around. We fed it twice a day, and that was the only interruption to its routine. It seemed happy enough. Every now and then, I'd be staring at it through the glass and it would stop and stare back. I always wondered whether it actually knew it was being watched. Did it know who I was, or was I just this color pattern that leaned in from time to time? It felt like my family was in the fishbowl now, but it was the opposite of the way it was with the goldfish. We were trapped, but had no idea for sure if we were being watched. We just acted like we were.

By lunchtime, we were all a little sick of each other. Nobody wanted to talk about why we were trapped, so we weren't talking about anything worth saying. After lunch, Mom told us to do our homework, and when we said it was all done, since we'd thought we'd be going to school today, she told us we had to do something educational—which in the end meant watching something from the documentary section of Netflix. Aidan picked a series about the Battle of the Bulge. I didn't argue.

The big excitement came around three o'clock when the doorbell rang again. Mom and Dad didn't even want to go to the peephole to see who it was, just in case it was a reporter who would know we were home. ("The family is at home, hiding behind a door right now," I imagined the reporter saying.) The doorbell rang again. Then there was knocking. Mom called the police, who got in touch with the squad car outside. There was a pause, and then Mom laughed.

"It's only Glenn," she told Dad.

We opened the door.

32

We went into the den, supposedly so Glenn could explain our homework assignments to us, but really, I suspected, so Glenn and Aidan could play a few games before Glenn had to go back home.

"I'm not really sure what the point is of me going around and getting this for you," Glenn said as he unpacked his bag and handed us some assignments. "All the teachers were like, 'This is what email is for, so we can send home assignments.' But I guess your parents still think it's the twentieth century or something."

"Maybe they just like your personal touch," Aidan joked, putting his assignments aside.

"Yeah, that must be it," Glenn said, sitting down on the couch. After he did, I saw him reach to his pocket and adjust his phone.

Aidan sat down next to him and loaded up a game. Casually, he asked, "So how was school today? What are they saying?"

Glenn shrugged. "I dunno, dude. Kelli was all like, 'My mom broke the story,' and I said, like real loud, 'Well, who wants a broken story, Kelli?' Even Keegan laughed at that one."

"Great," Aidan mumbled.

Glenn didn't notice Aidan was less than enthused—or if he did, he went on anyway. "Totally! I mean, you're a bigger mystery now than ever before, because you're, like, a *famous* mystery. Frances was saying she could imagine it on one of those programs like *CSI*. I mean, who do you want to be you in the movie version, right?"

"Let's just play."

For the first time I'd ever seen, Glenn tried to delay a game.

"Nah," he said, shifting on the couch and looking down at his phone again. "I want you to tell me what happened."

"Dude," Aidan said, "we've been through that."

"Yeah, but . . . I wasn't paying attention. I mean, there was a lot going on, right? So, like, tell me again what you told me before, about how this whole unicorn thing is a cover story for what *really* happened. You got lost in the woods, right? Then, like, stumbled your way home and were all out of your mind and came up with the story about the fantasy world. That's what you said."

Aidan, sitting next to him, couldn't see, but Glenn's hand went to his phone again. It was in his pocket, but the bottom was sticking out a little.

"Right?" Glenn pressed.

I jumped in and asked, "Are you *recording* this?"

"What are you talking about?" Glenn turned to me to protest. His hand went to his pocket again.

This time Aidan noticed. "What are you doing?" he asked.

"Nothing!" Glenn turned back to Aidan to say. While he was doing that, I swooped down and plucked the phone from his pocket.

The microphone was totally on. I held it up so Aidan could see.

"I wasn't—" Glenn sputtered.

But Aidan interrupted. "You totally were. Give me the phone, Lucas."

I did. He hit stop on the recording, then replayed the last few seconds.

"Give me the phone, Lucas."

Aidan hit delete, then handed Glenn's phone back to him.

"What's going on, Glenn?" he asked.

Glenn slumped back on the couch.

"I'm totally sorry," he said. "Honestly, I was thinking I could help you. Everyone's asking for the story, and there are so many reporters—like, decent reporters, not Kelli's mom—who would love to hear your side of the story."

You're kidding, right? I thought.

"You're kidding, right?" Aidan said.

Glenn threw up his hands. "Look—you have no idea how hard this has been. Like, everyone knows you're my best friend. So ever since you disappeared, everyone's been asking me about you. First about where you could've gone, and now about what the real story is. I get that you're saying you told me the real story and want me to keep it a secret. But what I don't understand is if it's the real story, why do you want to keep it a secret? Why aren't you telling everyone? Yeah, people will be all, 'Why can't he say where he was?' But at least they won't be calling you Unicorn Boy!"

"And they won't be calling you Unicorn Boy's best friend," Aidan added coolly.

"That's not my point!" Glenn said.

"Are you sure?" Aidan asked.

"Look, it was stupid to try to record you. Let's just play. We don't have to talk about it anymore."

Aidan looked at him for a second, then passed him a controller.

I wanted to kick Glenn out of the house. But it wasn't my call.

They played games for about an hour. Every now and then, Aidan would invite me to play too, taking one of their turns. So I stuck around.

Finally, Aidan finished a round and said, "I guess we better start that homework. Sorry, dude."

Glenn put his controller down. "No worries. I should probably head home anyway."

They said goodbye, and I almost asked to check Glenn's phone before he left. I had been watching him closely the whole time, but I might have missed it when I was playing—not that we'd been saying anything worth recording.

When Glenn was gone and Aidan and I were back in the den, I couldn't help myself. "I can't believe you let him stay!" I said.

Aidan spread his homework out in front of him. Then he looked up at me and replied, "If I'd kicked him out, he would've told everyone I kicked him out. He would've said he tried to get me to confess, and that I got angry at him instead. I'm not going to trust him, but I'm not going to cut him off either. Because if I cut him off, you know exactly where he'll go."

"That's sad," I said.

Aidan looked at me funny. Like, *What a strange thing for you to say.*

"I guess it is," he said finally. "But the saddest thing is that I'm not really surprised."

"Do you wish you were back there?"

Aidan shook his head, said, "That's a pointless question," and started on his homework even though there was no way of knowing if we'd be going to school the next day.

33

Even though we didn't talk about it, we all kept checking the news on our own devices. We typed Aidan's name into search engines to see if any new stories came up. A few local sites had picked up the story from the morning paper, but for the most part it stayed local, not viral.

The only acknowledgment that we were monitoring the outside as much as it was monitoring us came when six o'clock rolled around. Each of us took a local channel to watch, with Aunt Brandi tracking the internet. There hadn't been any more camera crews or reporters at our doorstep. And Julia, the press liaison, said she'd been getting fewer and fewer questions as the day went on, so we were hoping we'd be ignored.

There was a sewer main break. An exposé of the fruit flies that had descended on a Whole Foods. Traffic. Weather.

Nothing about unicorns.

Brandi called as soon as six-thirty hit and asked me to put it on speaker.

"How are you all doing?" she asked as we gathered for dinner.

"Ready to go for a jog," Dad said. "And I don't jog!"

"She knows you don't jog," Mom said. "Everyone who knows you knows you don't jog."

"Aidan?" Brandi asked.

"Couldn't be better!"

There was a pause. Then Brandi said, "I'll accept that on a grammatical technicality."

"I'll call you later," Mom said. "It's time to eat."

I hung up, but it was still another half hour before dinner was ready. Mom threw together what she called a "spontaneous potluck"—even I could tell we were eating whatever had been left in the fridge because my parents were afraid to go to the grocery store or have a delivery person at our door.

I was amazed that the phone didn't ring the whole time we had dinner. Then, after we were done, Mom said she'd check the messages, and I realized they'd turned off all of the ringers.

"It's best that way," Mom explained when I asked what was going on with the phones. "It's been a steady stream of nosy neighbors, crackpots, and every now and then a friend or relative who has no idea what to say."

I thought of all the people who'd been in our house the week Aidan was missing, up to the minute he returned. Back then, the way they'd shown support was to show up. Now they called or emailed. Although it was possible that Mom and Dad had told them to stay away.

After we were done with the dishes, Dad called another family meeting.

"We're returning to normal tomorrow," he announced. "You two are going to school, and Mom and I are going to work. Obviously, if anyone tries to talk to you about what happened, you don't say a word. And if anyone gives you any trouble in school, you go straight to the principal or the counselor. We talked to them earlier, and everyone's on board with this plan."

I was honestly relieved to hear we'd be leaving the fishbowl, even if it remained to be seen whether we'd have to wear smaller fishbowls to school.

Aidan didn't look relieved at all. "I don't want to go," he said.

Dad chuckled. "As with any other normal morning, you don't really have a choice, Aidan. You're going to school."

"I can't go back there," Aidan said.

And I realized: He wasn't talking about just tomorrow. He was talking about never going back again.

Dad didn't get it. He kept up his joking tone and said,

"Look, if I have to go to work, you have to go to school. That's the deal."

But Mom shook her head. She understood what Aidan was really saying.

"You want to go to a new school?" she asked.

Aidan nodded.

Dad appeared dumbstruck. "Look, I know it's rough, but—"

"It's never going to stop," Aidan said flatly. "We all know that."

Mom didn't miss a beat. "Is this about what happened?" she asked. "Or is this about *before* what happened? Has someone been giving you trouble at school?"

Aidan stood up from the table. "No. It's not about that at all."

"It's okay," Mom said carefully. "If that's why you ran away—"

"I didn't run away!" Aidan interrupted.

Dad slammed his hand down on the table. "Yes, you did. Let's be very clear about that, Aidan. No matter where you went, you *ran away.* You weren't kidnapped. Nobody forced you to leave. You left. Whether you stepped into another world or went to stay at a four-star hotel in Paris, it doesn't matter—you left us high and dry. No word. No warning. No trace. So you are going to sit back down and you are going to listen to whatever your mother and I have to say, and when we are through, you will do your homework, and then tomorrow morning, you will go to school. If, as your mother is asking, there was something that happened at school that led you to run away, we're all ears, and we will help you deal with it."

"I told you," Aidan said, sitting down, "there wasn't anything wrong."

"Let's keep it that way," Dad said.

Mom was staring at Dad, surprised. He never slammed his hand on the table or yelled. Now we all sat there, awkward. Dad had made Aidan stay for the rest of the conversation . . . but the conversation seemed over.

"It'll be good to get back to a routine," Mom said, but the sentence didn't lead to any other sentences.

Finally, since I knew Aidan wouldn't do it, I asked if we could be excused. Mom looked to Dad, and Dad said okay. He looked like he wanted to cry, or maybe yell again.

We left as quickly as we could.

34

The darkness of our bedroom, almost midnight.

"I didn't think of it as running away," Aidan said from his bed.

"Of course not," I said from mine.

"I was just taking a look. It's not like I thought I was going to stay."

"How could you?"

I tried to picture it, right above our heads. The light coming through the doors of the dresser. Opening it up. Seeing the green sky.

If that had happened to me, I would have gone in too.

Or.

Wouldn't I have come back downstairs first?

Wouldn't I have woken up Aidan, made him take a look to make sure I wasn't dreaming?

But Aidan had gone ahead without me.

"I wish you'd come to get me," I mumbled, sleepy.

"I didn't even think about it," Aidan said. Not apologetic. But honest. "I just went."

35

The next morning, Mom and Dad were taking the "normal routine" thing to heart. We had breakfast in our usual staggered way—me eating while Aidan showered, then me showering while Aidan ate. The radio on the counter was exhaling the news, and we weren't mentioned. Dad left for the office ten minutes before we left for school. Mom was still driving us; that was the one thing that had changed. They were still worried about us walking to school.

Nobody mentioned the police, or unicorns, or storytelling.

The phone didn't ring, but that didn't mean people weren't calling. We were just ignoring them for now.

This time when Glenn saw us arrive, he said, "Oh, wow—I didn't think you'd show up today."

"The classes in unicorn school were totally full, so I had to come back here," Aidan replied.

It took a beat for Glenn to start laughing—like he had to be sure Aidan was joking first.

Aidan was getting the celebrity stares again. I could see the effort it was taking to ignore them; I hoped no one else could tell.

When we got to his locker, we found someone had put unicorn stickers all across it. Some had already been scraped off, but a few remained.

"Very clever," Aidan commented. "So original."

"Yeah, pretty dumb," Glenn added.

Aidan got his books. My back was to the main entrance. So it was Glenn who saw the guy first. I noticed Glenn's expression getting confused, then turned to find this man who clearly didn't belong here. He wasn't old, maybe a college student, maybe a little older. He had a piece of paper in his hand, and with a shiver I realized it was the missing poster with Aidan's face on it.

"It's you," the guy said. "I found you again."

Aidan looked up. I didn't see any recognition in his eyes.

"Excuse me?" he said, tensing up.

"It's me. Zeke. You were there too. We were there together."

"I don't know what you're talking about," Aidan said.

The guy pushed forward, right next to him. Then he grabbed Aidan's shoulder.

"Hey!" Glenn said.

"We were there together," the guy said, his eyes somehow both wild and sincere. "In the land of Amber. When I saw the story in the paper, I knew. You came back to prepare for the merge, didn't you? You're another one of the advance troops."

People in the hallway were starting to stare now. "I'm getting help," Glenn said, running off. Aidan tried to shrug off Zeke's hand, but Zeke's grip held.

"I'm sorry," Aidan said. "I'm really sorry. But I think you're confused. I've never seen you before, here or anywhere else."

"NO!" Zeke shouted. "I know they told you to say that, but this is me. You're allowed to talk to *me*."

It was then that the first teacher, Mr. Thompson, got to us. Two seconds later, the lockdown siren started to blare. Kids went running into the nearest classrooms, barricading themselves inside.

"You don't want trouble," Mr. Thompson said to Zeke. "Let him go."

Zeke looked bewildered, but he raised his hands.

"He's lying," he told Mr. Thompson. "He knows me."

School security arrived, and while they surrounded

Zeke, Mr. Thompson gathered me and Aidan and walked us away.

LOCKDOWN! the mechanical voice of our alarm system blared through the empty halls. *LOCKDOWN!*

Instead of taking us to a classroom, Mr. Thompson led us to the main office. They put us in Principal Kahler's office with Vice Principal Ruiz while Mr. Thompson told everyone what had happened. As soon as Mr. Thompson walked out of the office, Vice Principal Ruiz locked the door.

"Don't worry," she told us. "We'll be safe here."

Through the principal's window, we could see the police cars show up, lights flashing. A few minutes later, we saw the police escort Zeke out. It looked like he was crying. He definitely wasn't putting up a fight.

"Poor Zeke," Aidan said.

This made Vice Principal Ruiz look up from her phone.

"You know his name?" she asked.

"He told it to us," I explained.

"Yeah," Aidan said. "That's the only way I know."

"Are you sure you've never seen him before?" the vice principal asked—a question we'd hear a lot in the next few hours.

"I'm positive," Aidan said. This answer would never change.

Zeke was put in the back of one of the police cars, and it drove away. Two other police cars stayed. As soon as the first car was out of the driveway, Principal Kahler went on the PA to say the lockdown was over, and that it had been a false alarm. First period would start in five minutes, and would be shortened today so we could resume a regular class schedule.

Through the window we could see other cars pulling into the driveway now, adults getting out.

"Parents," Vice Principal Ruiz explained. "No doubt, some of the students texted their parents about the lockdown. So they're coming to see what's happening, to make sure their kids are okay. It's going to be a mess. I'm going to go out there, but you two stay here, okay?"

It hadn't occurred to either me or Aidan to text our parents. But within a half hour, they were in the principal's office with us, having been called by the school secretary.

Mom arrived first, hugging us close and checking us for any damage.

"Are you okay?" she kept asking. "Really, are you okay?"

Dad, when he got there, was more angry than anything else.

"I hope they lock that guy away. Storming into a school and assaulting a child."

"Now, Jim . . . ," Mom said.

"No," Dad replied. "I mean it."

"He was just confused," Aidan said quietly. "He honestly believed I'd been with him in the land of Amber, whatever that is. He wasn't trying to hurt me. He was just . . . glad to have found someone else."

"Please," Dad said, "don't defend him. What he did was wrong, Aidan. They had to lock down the whole school!"

Mom shook her head. "I just wish I'd known that the people who left those messages might actually show up. I thought we were being pranked. Now I know."

People. I noticed that she'd said *people,* plural.

Principal Kahler came in then, along with Officer Pinkus, Vice Principal Ruiz, and Mr. Lemon, the guidance counselor.

Officer Pinkus asked us to tell them what happened, so we did. At one point, they called Glenn and Mr. Thompson out of class so they could say what they'd seen too. Then they were let go, and it was just our family again with the administrators and the officer.

Mom launched in with, "What I don't understand is how this could happen. How can a madman just walk into this school and find my son?"

Principal Kahler was ready for this question, and explained that the school security guards had been distracted by a scuffle between students, leaving the front doors "momentarily unguarded." This just happened to coincide with Aidan's arrival at school; the speculation was that Zeke had been waiting the whole time for Aidan to get there. When he saw Aidan, he followed him in.

"This is a highly unusual situation," Principal Kahler added. "But we will make sure this never happens again."

Nobody asked why it was "highly unusual." It had been one thing when Aidan had been a missing kid. Now there was another layer on top of that, and nobody knew what to do with that layer.

As if sensing this, Aidan said, "I'm sorry."

"There's no reason to be sorry," Officer Pinkus said at the same time that Mr. Lemon asked, "For what?"

Aidan chose to answer Mr. Lemon. "For opening my mouth in the first place," he said.

You were only telling the truth, I wanted someone to say. But Dad just nodded. Mom reached over and patted Aidan on the shoulder. Principal Kahler and Vice Principal Ruiz gave each other a look. Officer Pinkus studied Aidan.

And I . . . well, I didn't say anything either.

It was the middle of third period by the time we were told we could go back to class.

"Are you sure that's a good idea?" Mom asked.

Both Officer Pinkus and Principal Kahler assured her we'd be safe. Security had our class schedules and would be close by at all times. And at least one patrol car would always be in the driveway, to signal a police presence.

I wondered, though, if Mom's question was about more

than just our physical safety. I wondered if she had some sense of what it would be like for us to go back to class after all that had happened.

The principal was actually going to have the security guards escort us to class, but Aidan said, "Please, no," and a compromise was reached, that they would follow us discreetly, but not parade us into class in front of everyone else.

Still, everyone knew. That was clear the minute I walked into math class. The teacher knew. All the other students knew. Even the cutouts of Alan Turing and Albert Einstein on the bulletin board looked like they knew.

But we all pretended it was normal, that I was late to class for a normal reason.

Busby was seated on the other side of the room, and I could see her buzzing to talk to me. Tate was closer, but he was much more inclined to be worried about being caught talking in class. So it wasn't until the bell rang and class was over that the two of them unloaded everything they had to say.

Not surprisingly, Busby did most of the talking as we walked to fourth period.

"They're saying that your brother was almost kidnapped! That maybe the person who kidnapped him the first time came back. Or it was another kidnapper. And if Glenn hadn't run for Mr. Thompson, the crazy kidnapper might have gotten him. That's what a lot of people are saying. Other people are saying this guy was your brother's accomplice when he ran away, and that they came up with the unicorn story together. But that doesn't really make sense. Oh, and Kelli McGillis was trying to call her mother to give her all the details and Ms. Walters confiscated her phone, which caused Kelli to throw a total fit, so now she has detention. I thought you'd like that part."

"It wasn't a kidnapper," I told Busby and Tate. "It was just some sad guy who thought he knew my brother but didn't."

Busby sighed. "I know. But I'm just telling you what other people are saying."

"Let us know what we can do," Tate added. "Not about this, but about . . . everything."

He left it at that, and I appreciated that unlike other people throughout the day, my friends didn't ask me to explain any more. They were there for me whether or not they had a full explanation, because I was their friend.

I didn't see Aidan again until the end of school. He was waiting at my locker for me. Glenn was nowhere in sight.

"You already got your books?" I asked as I figured out mine.

"Yeah," he said. "I decided it would be better to wait here than wait outside."

"How did it go today?"

"It went."

I smiled. "Be more specific?"

Aidan shrugged. "Kelli blamed me for the lockdown, and said that it could have been avoided if I'd stayed home. Trinity, this other girl in our class, pointed out that the psycho—her word, not mine—wouldn't have known about my story if Kelli's mom hadn't put it in the paper. Then Keegan had to defend Kelli and said that the whole thing was me crying for attention, and the best thing everyone could do was ignore me. I wanted to agree with him, but didn't want to call attention to myself."

"Sounds like a great day," I said, pulling my book bag onto my shoulder and slamming my locker.

"Well," Aidan said, surprising me, "I think Zeke's day was probably worse."

Busby found us then, and chatted about something that had nothing to do with Aidan, and then we were in the car with Mom, who kept asking if everything had been okay with the rest of our day. It wasn't until we were back in our room, just the two of us, that I got to talk more with Aidan about what had happened.

"Were you scared?" I asked.

"Yes. But do you want to know the truth?"

I nodded.

Aidan went over to our door and closed it before continuing.

"Okay," he said quietly. "Here's the thing. For about five seconds, I was excited. I thought that maybe Zeke had been in Aveinieu, and if he had been there, then it would prove to everyone else that I had been there too. It wasn't until he mentioned the land of Amber and the plot to merge worlds that I was like, *Oh, this guy doesn't know Aveinieu at all. He's lost in another world.* That's when I wanted to get out of there. But let me tell you—if he'd said the word *Aveinieu,* if he'd been able to tell me back a little of what I saw there . . . he would have been my new best friend."

"But he was crazy!" I said.

"As crazy as I am?" Aidan asked.

"No. You're not crazy at all."

"But maybe he *did* go somewhere else. Maybe the land of Amber exists. Who are we to say? It's just not the same place I went to."

What Aidan was telling me scared me. Because I imagined him older, being just like Zeke, if he held on to Aveinieu the same way Zeke held on to whatever world he believed he'd been to.

"That isn't going to be you," I said.

Aidan shrugged again. "I hope not. But right now, that definitely seems like one of the paths."

I didn't know what to say to that, at least not at first. It wasn't until Aidan had swooped up his laptop and gone to the attic to do his work that I thought to say, "Well, figure out how to stay on one of the other paths. Please."

36

Dad was late for dinner, and in a bad mood when he got there.

"I had to stay at work because of the disruption this morning," he explained as he sat down, even though nobody had asked for an explanation. Then, worse, he added, "It's unclear to my boss whether any of this is covered by our attendance policy. I told him, fine, I'd take it as a vacation day. And he actually had the nerve to tell me the precise number of vacation days I had left."

"He was so understanding when Aidan was missing," Mom said. "He told you not to worry about it."

"Well," Dad said, pushing over the silverware to free his napkin, "that seems to have changed."

"That doesn't make sense," Mom said.

"Doesn't it?" Dad replied.

It was like they'd forgotten Aidan and I were there. Until Aidan put down his fork and said it again: "I'm sorry."

"It's fine," Mom said.

But Aidan looked at Dad and said, "Obviously it's not."

Dad started to serve himself. As he did, he told us, "Look, the point here is that my boss is more of a jerk than I thought. That's it."

Let it go, I tried to signal Aidan. He'd been eating his chicken without seeming too disgusted with it. I wanted him to go back to that.

But he pressed on.

"No, this is all my fault. Everything. I know that."

"It's not your fault," Dad said.

"But it is! You said it yourself last night. I ran away. And, even worse, I ran away to a place you don't actually believe exists. I wish you hadn't forced me to tell you. I wish I could have thought of a better story in time. But I couldn't. So I told you the truth, and you don't believe it."

"Stop," Dad said.

"What?" Aidan jutted out his chin defiantly. "Are you saying you believe me?"

"We're trying to believe you," Mom offered. "Truly. We are."

Aidan shook his head. "But you never ask me about it. Lucas is the only one who does. You just want to hear me say something else."

"We're being patient!" Dad said, too loud. "We're giving you space to get to the point where you can tell us what really happened."

Mom jumped in. "What he means is that we'll listen to whatever you want to say. Whether it's about Aveinieu or somewhere else."

Aidan stood up. "You don't want to hear any of it. Either you'll think I'm lying or you'll think I'm like Zeke. I don't like those choices."

"Sit back down and eat," Dad said.

But this time it didn't work.

"I'm not hungry anymore," Aidan said. Then he left the room.

"Get back here!" Dad yelled after him, moving to get up himself.

Mom stopped him, holding out a hand to gesture him in place.

"Let him blow off some steam," she said. "It's been a hard day for all of us. And if this is what he needs to do, let him do it."

We heard his footsteps. Up to our room. Then farther up to the attic.

I wondered what we would have done if he'd gone for the front door.

37

I wasn't sure he'd want to see me, so after dinner I went to our room instead of the attic. I could hear his movements: sitting down, standing up. Then it went still for about five minutes and I thought, *This is ridiculous.* I wasn't getting anything done. I was waiting for him.

So I went up to the attic.

He wasn't on his laptop. His books were closed. Instead, he was sitting in front of the dresser.

Its doors were open. It was still empty.

He turned to me when I came in, but didn't really change his expression.

"What are you doing?" I asked.

"Thinking."

"About what?"

I was hovering over him, not sure where to go. He

180

pointed to the space next to him on the floor, which was more of an invitation than I expected. I sat down.

"About what to do," he said.

That was meant to be the answer. I didn't sense he wanted me to ask another question. But I asked anyway.

"What to do about what?"

"I don't know how to make it go away."

He wasn't looking at me when he said this. He was both looking at the dresser and looking at the world beyond the dresser. Not Aveinieu. Our world. Our judging world.

"It's all my fault," he said again sadly.

He wasn't sitting on the spot where I'd found him; I was. I remembered that moment. Remembered the frantic minutes after. It was such a rush. Now I slowed it down, thought about it.

"Actually, it's all my fault," I said. Before Aidan could protest—I think he was going to protest—I pushed on. "You didn't tell them anything. Or maybe you wouldn't have. But I told them. I shouldn't have told them. I should have kept my mouth shut. If I hadn't told them, none of this would have happened."

Now Aidan looked at me hard. "True. But honestly? There wasn't anything else for me to tell them. I don't think I would've been able to make anything else up on the spot."

"Maybe not. But eventually. If we'd put it off, you might have come up with something else."

Aidan sighed and leaned on the old chest that once belonged to our great-great-grandparents.

"Back there," he said, "we kept telling each other, 'Nobody back home would ever believe this.' It was like this running joke, anytime something incredible happened. And even if I wasn't saying it out loud, I was thinking it in my head. They have these fireflies that come out at night, but instead of being one color, they blink in all these different colors, talking to each other. The first time I saw them in the sky, all these blips and bursts, it was like a light show or a video game, and I thought, 'Lucas would never believe this. I wish Lucas could see this.' It wasn't like my mind left here entirely. But I knew that unless you came into the world with me, there was no way to believe it. You always read a lot and have so much more of an imagination than I do—but even you would have had a hard time."

He looked at the dresser again. "I talked to Cordelia about it, and she said she still thought that way, even though she knew that most of her family and friends would be gone now, back in our world. 'It keeps them alive,' she said. 'Thinking about them.' And that scared me a little, thinking that even though I'd only been gone a short time, you were already a different Lucas than the one I'd left, and you'd continue to become a different Lucas, even if in my mind you'd always be the same as when I left. And then, when they told me I had to go back, that they were worried I'd brought a sickness with me, I had no idea what I'd find. Nobody had ever gone back and forth before—we didn't know whether it was because they weren't able to or didn't want to. So I didn't know if I was coming back two seconds after I left or two hundred years. Or if I'd come back at all. I asked Cordelia, 'What do I tell them?' And she said she had no idea. She'd never done what I was about to do."

He turned back to me. "You kind of know the rest. I came back. You found me. The moment I saw the attic, I knew not much had changed, but it wasn't until you came in that I knew I hadn't been gone that long. And while I was still really sad about being forced to leave, I was also grateful that at least you were still here."

"And I was grateful you were back!" I told him.

That made him smile. "Thanks. It was cool that everyone was so happy. I wish we could have stayed there, you know?"

"People are still happy you're back. Mom and Dad especially."

"I know. But it's gotten so messy. And I wish I could unmess it."

"But you're telling the truth."

Aidan smiled, but this time it didn't look as happy. He leaned into me and said, "Yeah, but the truth isn't very helpful if people don't believe it. Or at least that's what it looks like now. I mean, it's started to play with my mind too. There are times when I wonder if it was all this really intense dream, that I was lost somewhere, came back here, and my mind is trying really hard to forget where it was, so it's made up this other experience out of dream material. What if everyone else is right? What if I'm making all of this up?"

"But there was the leaf," I pointed out.

"Oh yeah. The leaf." Aidan leaned back on the chest again. "The crumpled, brown leaf."

"It was blue. I saw it. It wasn't from here."

"And is that why you believe me? Because of a single leaf?"

I thought about my answer; I knew Aidan wanted me to. Then I shook my head and said, "No. I believe it because you believe it too."

"It's weird how much that helps. To have one other person know the truth. To have that reflecting back at me. I don't actually need the world to know. Just one or two people."

"Well, count me in."

"We just have to figure out something to tell everyone else," Aidan said.

I took it as a challenge.

In my mind, I started to explore the options.

38

We tried normal again the next day, and did better at it.

Mom and Dad kept their distance at breakfast and didn't mention dinner. Mom reminded Aidan he had another therapist appointment after school, and he said he remembered. Then Mom told me I'd have to come along, because Dad couldn't get out of work to pick me up. I could have tried to convince her I could walk home alone, but decided it wasn't worth it. I said I was fine going along.

At school, there was more security at the doors. But once we walked in, it was like everyone had decided the joke wasn't funny anymore, and had moved on. The stickers were gone from Aidan's locker. We got some weird looks, but not too many. Aidan searched out Glenn and the rest of their friends, and they all volleyed words around like nothing had happened. Seeing this, I realized that Aidan was lucky—he'd never been a jerk to people, so people weren't inclined to be jerks back to him when he was vulnerable. They liked him, and liking would forgive a lot.

There was still some snark, but it was containable. When Kelli McGillis tried to call Aidan "Unicorn Boy" again, Glenn said, "Hey, how about we start calling you Vulture Girl?" Apparently, word spread, and by lunch, kids were walking over to Kelli and saying, "Is that seat next to you available, Vulture Girl?" By the fifth time, she was like, "Alright, I get it. Stop."

Another thing that helped Aidan: He hadn't done anything to anyone else, only to himself.

As far as my friends were concerned, Tate and Truman were happy to change the subject—only Busby kept asking me if I'd learned more about what had *really* happened.

"He ran away, okay?" I said. "He wishes he hadn't done it. Now he's back, and if that's all that matters to my family, then that should be all that matters to my friends, right?"

"Okay," Busby replied. "It's just that Aidan disappearing was the most interesting thing that has ever happened here. Now we're going to have to go back to talking about boring things."

"I'm okay with boring," I told her.

I welcomed boring.

I didn't hear anything Aidan said to the therapist—
I guess therapists make sure to have walls and doors thick
enough that the people in the waiting room can't hear a
word.

Mom had her laptop with her and was doing work. I
was supposed to be doing my homework. But I think both
of us kept stopping to look at the door to the therapist's office, wondering about what Aidan was saying inside.

"It's going to be okay," I told Mom when I caught her
looking.

She turned to me, surprised by what I'd said.

"Why do you think so?" she asked. Not arguing, but
curious.

"Aidan's not going anywhere," I told her. "If that's what
you and Dad are worried about, you don't have to worry
about it."

"Oh, Lucas," Mom said, putting her hand on my arm,
"that *is* what we're worried about. And I'm sure we'll keep
worrying about it. But it's good to hear you say we don't
have to. We'll get through this, I'm sure."

I'd been trying to make her feel better, but she made
me feel better too.

It felt like we were all on the same side again.

At the same time, Aidan had given me an assignment, and I kept thinking about it: Where could he say he'd gone, besides Aveinieu?

Aunt Brandi called me to check in, and I told her the day had gone well—the therapist had told Mom that Aidan seemed like he was in a good place, even with all the strange circumstances. I liked that phrase, *strange circumstances*, as if it was something that had been sprung on Aidan, not something he had sprung on us. Brandi said she liked that phrase too.

"But how are *you*, Lucas? I don't want you to think that we're all so caught up in Aidan's feelings that we don't care about yours."

"I'm fine," I told her. "Aidan's actually talking to me more than he did before. I like that."

"That's good," Brandi said. She didn't ask me what Aidan was saying, like Mom or Dad would have. I appreciated that.

After I hung up, I thought about how Brandi had been away in Peru when Aidan had gone missing. *What if he went to see her and she wasn't there?* I thought. I just needed a reason for Aidan to go there, because it wasn't like he'd sneak out in the middle of the night to visit our aunt, no matter how cool she was. What if Aidan and I had gotten into a big fight and he'd stormed off? But that didn't make sense. What could I have possibly said to Aidan to make him leave like that? Nobody would believe it, especially not Mom and Dad. No, I figured, Aidan had to be running away *to* something, not away from here.

I thought about things Aidan liked, and the best I could do was gaming. So I went online and typed in *gaming* and the name of Brandi's city and the day Aidan had disappeared. It didn't take me long to find a gaming convention that was going on the weekend he was gone.

I explored some more and made notes in my head.

When I was done, I erased my trail.

39

I waited until we had gone to bed and Mom and Dad were safely in their room. I knew Officer Pinkus was coming to see Aidan the next day, Friday. And I figured that would be a good time for him to premiere the new story I'd made him.

"Are you ready for it?" I asked.

"Wait," he said. Then he came and sat on the foot of my bed. "Okay, tell me."

So I told him about the gaming convention. He could say he'd wanted to go but knew Mom and Dad would never let him. (True.) So he snuck out of the house. He figured when he got to the city, he'd go to Aunt Brandi's and she'd put him up. But when he got there, no one answered. (He'd just have to say he'd forgotten when she was leaving for Peru.) And he'd left behind his phone, so he couldn't call her, and didn't know her number by heart, so couldn't call from someone else's phone. (Also possible.)

Aidan started with his questions.

Why didn't I have my phone? Wouldn't I have known I'd need it?

You were afraid they'd trace it.

And how did I get to the city? Did I take the train? The bus?

You took the train. But you waited until rush hour. That way, no one would see you on the security cameras. I'm pretty sure they checked the security cameras.

So what did I do when I got to the city, after I found out Brandi wasn't there?

You went to the hotel where the convention was.

In my pajamas?

No. You brought clothes. Old clothes that we didn't notice were missing. And a costume! Yeah, you had kept a costume. Which made it hard for you to be recognized.

So where did I stay?

The convention was in a hotel. So maybe you just slept on the couches there.

Or maybe there was a park nearby.

I guess. But Mom and Dad won't like the thought that you slept in a park.

Okay. So I found a space in the hotel.

Yeah.

And then what?

I think you realized what kind of trouble you'd be in. After a few days.

So why didn't I call home?

This was the tricky part.

You did call home.

What?

I was the one who picked up. There were times when Mom was busy and Dad was out looking. So it's possible I picked up the phone.

Lucas, you can't say that.

Why not?

You know why not. You'll be in so much trouble.

I know.

You can't.

I have to. That's the only way the story makes sense.

Aidan looked at me for a second, and it didn't seem like I'd convinced him. Still, he was willing to hear it out.

So what did you say to me?

I told you people were freaking out.

Then why didn't you tell everyone I was on the phone? You could have ended it right there!

Because you begged me not to. You said you'd come home as long as I didn't tell anyone. Since I wanted you to come home, I promised.

And I trusted you.

Well, you didn't tell me where you were. But you said you'd get home.

So I got on the next train. . . .

Not yet. Because you still had two days to go. Let's say you were leaving your bag where you were sleeping, and while you were away and thought it was safe, it got stolen. Or maybe just your money was stolen, since your pajamas couldn't have been stolen.

You're scarily good at this.

Thanks. So you have your bag, but you don't have a ticket or money to get a ticket. So it takes you a day or two to get enough money to come home.

How do I get the money?

Just by asking people. You stick to the hotel. Say your parents are gone for the day and you got locked out of your room.

Why didn't I ask for a new key?

There was a misunderstanding. They checked out. And now you need cab fare to get to where they are.

So I get the money, and get a train back.

You call me from the train station. Maybe hang up a few times when Mom or Dad picks up. But when you get me, you tell me when the train gets in. I figure out how long it will take for you to walk from the station. Along the way, you come up with the story about going to another world—you know it makes no sense, but you figure no one will be able to prove it or disprove it. And you can't think of anything else.

That's a stretch.

Anything we come up with is a stretch.

Okay. So I get home . . .

Well, we come up with a signal—when the adults are all busy, I go into the backyard and signal you to come out of the woods. Then I sneak you up to the attic. You hide there until I come "find" you.

They didn't search the attic the day I was found?

No. They'd already done it a few times. It would have never occurred to them that you'd sneak back in and hide there.

Because I'd need an accomplice.

I guess so. I was your accomplice.

My story ended there. Aidan was back home. He'd hoped to get away with not saying where he'd been, but then I slipped, and he had to tell them his cover story, about Aveinieu.

I thought Aidan would congratulate me on coming up with an alternative to what everyone thought. But instead of congratulations, he said, "I have to think about this." Then he went back to his own bed.

I was a little disappointed. Then, out of the dark of our room, there came a "Thank you," and the disappointment went away.

40

At breakfast the next morning, Mom and Dad announced they'd turned the ringers back on. But if the phone rang, we still weren't supposed to pick it up unless we knew the name on the caller ID.

"Hopefully the attention is dying down," Dad told us.

"We'll see," Mom said.

I was nervous the whole day at school, thinking about the conversation with Officer Pinkus that was going to happen in the afternoon—if Aidan decided to go through with it. I'd told him I figured Officer Pinkus was the best person to start with. If she said our story made sense, then everyone else would think so, starting with our parents. I knew they'd be mad at us at first, but I figured eventually it would be okay. They'd much rather have a son who ran off to a gaming convention than a son who ran off to another world.

I only had a few minutes with Aidan after school.

"So what did you decide?" I asked.

"I think it's worth trying," he said.

"Should we practice?"

Aidan shook his head. "Not enough time."

Once we were in Mom's car, on the way home, there wasn't any way to talk about it any further.

Officer Pinkus showed up at four o'clock. I was relieved to see there weren't any other officers with her.

"As promised, just a check-in," she assured my parents. "We haven't seen any other unusual activity. Mr. Risen is now back in his care facility and knows not to enter any other schools." It took me a moment to realize that Mr. Risen was Zeke.

After Mom and Dad made some small talk with Officer Pinkus, she suggested we all sit down.

"Actually," Aidan said, "can Lucas and I talk to you alone for a moment?"

All the adults in the room seemed surprised by this, but Mom and Dad let Officer Pinkus take the lead.

"Sure," she said. "Where should we go?"

"How about the attic?" Aidan suggested.

Mom and Dad exchanged a glance. But Officer Pinkus was already leading the way.

Aidan and I followed.

41

Aidan sat on the chest. I sat on the floor. Officer Pinkus sat on the edge of the rocking chair, so it wouldn't rock. The dresser stood in its usual place.

"I have something to tell you," Aidan said. Then he corrected, "*We* have something to tell you."

I thought this meant I'd share some of the storytelling. But once Aidan started, he didn't leave any room for me. He started by explaining to her how much he loved gaming, about how excited he'd been to go to the gaming convention—and how sure he'd been that his parents wouldn't let him go during school. From there, he told the whole story, just as we'd put it together the night before. Officer Pinkus took some notes, but mostly she listened.

"I'm really sorry I lied," he said at the end. "It started out with me doing something wrong, and then it just got worse and worse. I didn't mean to scare so many people. I feel awful about it."

"I'm sorry too," I added. "For what I did."

"I see," Officer Pinkus said, putting her notebook aside. "Now do you mind if I ask you a few questions?"

"Sure," Aidan said, totally calm.

"Okay. Let me start with this one: How did you call home, Aidan?"

Aidan's calm edged a little further away. "What do you mean?"

"You left your phone here. How did you call home?"

"I used a phone at the hotel."

"Where in the hotel?"

"Where there were phones? Like, public phones."

"Are you saying there are pay phones in the hotel?"

"Yeah."

"You're sure I'll find pay phones there?"

Aidan nodded.

"And when I check the records for those pay phones, I'll find calls to this house."

"Yes," Aidan said. But it sounded like he was saying it because he had to.

"What costume did you bring?"

"What?"

"You said you went in costume. What was the costume?"

"Um . . . Super Mario?"

"You wore the same costume every day."

"Yes?"

"And did you shower?"

"No?"

"You said your wallet was stolen?"

"Yes."

"Then how did we find your wallet in your room while you were gone?"

"He had a second wallet!" I jumped in when it looked like Aidan didn't have an answer.

"Okay, look," Officer Pinkus said. "I could very easily check every aspect of your story. Phone records. Security footage at the hotel. I could talk to the organizers of this convention and see if there was any way in without a badge; I'm guessing the answer's no. Or, Aidan, I could ask you to describe the convention and the hotel. You were there for three or four days, after all. I'm sure you can tell me all about it."

Aidan seemed to be shrinking into the shadows. He wasn't going to say no, but he had also run out of yes.

Officer Pinkus rocked forward to us.

"Here's the thing—you seemed much, much more genuine when you were talking about Aveinieu. Even though most people think it's impossible, I believe that much more than I believe what you're saying now. I'm sure you have your reasons, and I can probably guess at what those reasons are, but for a minute I need the old Aidan back, the one who wasn't lying to me. Do you understand?"

Aidan nodded.

"I'm going to ask you two questions again. And you need to give me the honest answers. First, were you kidnapped?"

"No," Aidan said clearly.

"Second, even if you weren't kidnapped, did you leave here to meet up with anyone?"

"No."

"Nobody helped you."

"No."

"Not even Lucas?"

Aidan shook his head. "Not even Lucas. I ran away. I was alone. And then I came back. Alone."

Now it was Officer Pinkus who nodded. Then she sat back for a second, decided something, and rocked again toward us.

"When I was fourteen," she said, "my older sister ran away. She did it to be with a boy who wasn't good for her. We'd all warned her about him; she wouldn't listen. So she left, and it ended very badly. I never saw her again. Which is why I do what I do . . . and why you need to listen to me now. Got it?"

"Got it," Aidan and I both said.

"Good. As long as no one hurt you, the only thing that

matters now is that you're back. And the only thing that matters going forward is that you don't run away again. This doesn't just matter to me; it matters to your parents, your town, your friends. Stay here. And if you ever get the feeling you want to run away again, talk to someone about it. Because running away without a word is never going to be the answer to your problems; it will only cause more problems. There are certainly kids out there who need to be in a better place than the home they've been given— but you're not one of those kids. You are a kid who is surrounded by love. You might not see it all the time—none of us ever do. But it's there. Whenever you need to reach for it, reach for it, because it's there. Do you feel that?"

"Yes," Aidan said.

"And do you promise not to disappear again?" Officer Pinkus gestured toward the dresser. "For whatever reason."

Aidan didn't look to the dresser. He looked straight at Officer Pinkus.

"I promise."

She stood up then and told us, "As far as I'm concerned, this case is now closed. I will tell your parents that. I will say that to anyone who asks. I loathe the fact that it was our lapse that put your story out there in the first place. But now it's yours again, and you don't have to do anything else with it if you don't want to. If you end up having more to tell me, my door will always be open to you. Never make up things because you think they're what people want to hear. Most of the time when you do that, you end up being wrong."

Aidan and I stood up too. Officer Pinkus offered her hand, and one after the other, we shook it.

Before she left the attic, she took a look around, then said to us, "There's no place like home, right?"

And we agreed.

There's no place like home.

42

True to her word, Officer Pinkus told Mom and Dad that the case was closed and they needed to start treating it that way too.

"What's important is that he's back," she said. And they repeated it.

The fact that it didn't matter where he'd been was unspoken, but understood.

Aidan and I had an intense conversation before bed that night, and over the next few weeks talking before bed became something like a tradition. Not about Aveinieu, but about other things. Once I'd proven my belief in him, it carried over to other things. Which made life easier for both of us, to be able to talk about it.

He stayed friends with Glenn, but not really best

friends. His friend group grew pretty big, and even included Kelli and Keegan. Every now and then, someone made a unicorn joke, but mostly people stayed away from it. It was too weird, too unusual to deal with. So it stopped being what they thought about when they thought about Aidan. He tried to do lots of other things—he joined track, started singing in the school chorus—to define himself more.

About a month after the case was closed, Mom and Dad drove us into the city for a day with Aunt Brandi. She'd found a gamer con that she thought Aidan and I would like, one that was aimed at teens and kids. It was actually thrown by the same organization as the one Aidan had pretended to go to, in the same hotel. Of course, Brandi had no way of knowing that. She also didn't understand why we were on the hunt for pay phones.

We didn't find any.

But Aidan did find something else. Because two of Brandi's friends came along with their own kids. And one of those kids was a boy Aidan's age named Luther. From the moment they started talking, it was clear they weren't going to stop talking anytime soon. Luther even joined us on the pay phone hunt, without needing to know why we were so desperate to find one.

After we got back home, Aidan and Luther started texting and gaming together. After three weeks, they were dating, and suddenly Aidan was known as the seventh grader with a gamer boyfriend who lived in the city. People talked about it for a week, and then it seemed like it had always been the case.

I hung out with Busby, Tate, and Truman as usual, and unicorns never came up again. The next time they were over at my house, they definitely were curious to see the attic. But I think that curiosity died out when they found an ordinary dresser in an ordinary attic. It must have been much more interesting in their imaginations.

I started to do my homework up there. Aidan had pretty much claimed the den as his after-school domain, and I wanted a domain of my own. It was nice and quiet up above everything else.

It was about two months after Officer Pinkus had sat in the rocking chair that I stretched out on the floor to do some math problems and noticed that the pages on my notebook were moving. Just the wind—but not just the wind. Because it wasn't coming from the open door to downstairs.

It was coming from the dresser.

43

I stood up.

Walked forward.

The wind was unmistakable, emanating from the crack between the doors. I expected them to swing open at any moment.

I looked into the crack and saw green.

This can't be happening, I thought.

And if it wasn't happening, it wouldn't matter if I opened the doors.

So I did.

And there it was.

The sky wasn't just green—it was like seeing an emerald from the inside, with the light glimmering through. There were hills in the distance, but they seemed to be leaning toward me, defying any sense they might have had of gravity. They were more like horns than hills, really, one shade darker than a plum and one shade lighter than a shadow. The ground itself seemed to have veins running through it, thin stripes that might have been roads or might have been rows of red and blue trees.

This was Aveinieu, right in front of me. I had no doubt.

I was looking out onto it as if I were in a tower rising above the landscape. When I leaned in and looked down, I saw a wall that looked like the inside of an oyster, smooth to the touch. And against it was what could only be called a cross between a ladder and a staircase, a temporary structure allowing me to step into the new world.

I looked for people, for animals, for any sign of life. But if they were out there watching, they were hiding well.

Mom and Dad weren't home yet—they'd gone back to letting us walk home from school.

But Aidan was home. Just downstairs. In the den.

I made a move to get him. . . .

And stopped.

Because just as I started toward the stairs, the wind changed.

It was no longer blowing out.

It was drawing me in.

And I asked myself: *What do you want?*

The answer wasn't: *I want to leave.*

It wasn't: *I want everyone to know.*

It was: *I don't want anything to change.*

Aidan was happy now. He had friends, a boyfriend, a life. Our family had been disrupted by Aveinieu, and then we'd made it through the disruption.

There's no going back.

The wind felt stronger. My pencil skidded across the floor, the notebook following more slowly, and the textbook slower still. The rocking chair nodded, then pulled away.

I knew what I had to do. Or at least I felt I knew what I had to do, which was enough.

I reached down for the pencil and ripped a page out of the notebook.

He's not coming back, I wrote. *He's happy here.*

Then I folded the page into a paper airplane and launched it into the green sky.

I stood there in my attic and watched it soar far beyond the back of the dresser, far into somewhere I'd never go, drifting and drifting until I couldn't see it any longer.

Then I shut the doors.

The wind slowed down. The green edged back to black.

Five minutes later, I opened the doors and found the empty dresser again.

Ten minutes after that, Aidan called up to me.

Not because he'd felt something or heard something.

No. He just wanted to see if I wanted to play a game.

44

A week later, the dresser was gone, along with a few other attic things we never used.

"Your father was having nightmares about it," Mom said over dinner that night.

Dad put his fork down and said, "Your mother also announced she was getting tired of the clutter."

"Who'd you give it to?" I asked.

"We didn't give it to anyone," Dad said. "We threw it out."

Aidan didn't say a word. But really, it wasn't Aidan I was studying. It was our father.

Why now? What did you see? I wanted to ask him.

But I couldn't do it without giving us both away.

45

The night we'd given Officer Pinkus our false story, only to have it dismissed, Aidan and I returned to our bedroom, back to the real story. Once again, we talked in nighttime darkness, right before our minds would take us into the realm of sleep.

"We were really bad at that," Aidan said from his bed. "But thanks anyway."

"Anytime," I said.

He laughed. "But hopefully never again."

"But hopefully never again," I agreed.

I thought that was the end of the conversation. But a minute later, Aidan said, "I'm worried."

"That Officer Pinkus will tell?"

"No. I'm worried that I'll forget."

I didn't have to ask *Forget what?* I knew.

Aidan went on. "I worry that the more time goes by, the

more it will feel like a dream, like something that didn't happen. I worry I'll forget what it was like. Especially if I never get the chance to go back there, I would like to remember what it was like to see a green sky and to feed a maddox and to drink plenty tea and to stand next to Cordelia and see the sun set. I want to remember what it was like to be so far away from here. But how can I?"

"Tell me everything you remember," I said. "And I'll try to remember it too."

So we talked, quietly and for hours.

At the end, I promised again that we would share this, because I believed every word. That I would remember.

And I have. I have held on to this story. It's not something I think about all the time. I can go long stretches without thinking about it. But every now and then I'll remember, and every now and then Aidan and I will remember together. Sometimes we'll talk about it when no one else is around. But more often than not, it's just a look we share. Or I'll feel something, that shiver of memory, and I'll turn to see that Aidan is feeling it too.

We don't tell it to each other much anymore, but the story is still there. Like all honest stories, it lives within us.

True or not, every story has something it wants you to remember.

True or not, every story has something it wants you to believe.

ACKNOWLEDGMENTS

Many, many people helped this *Disappearance* appear. Thanks to my friends, some of whom make appearances in this book as authority figures, which can't possibly be right. Thanks as well to Billy, Nick, and Anica, who were the first friends to hear its beginning aloud.

Thanks to my parents, who were gracious in letting me make up worlds (as long as I didn't disappear into them), and to my brother (for never going missing for six hours, not to mention six days).

Thank you to everyone at Random House Children's Books, in particular Melanie, Mary, and Barbara for their enthusiasm about me stepping into a new place, and April and Carol for envisioning the cover. And thanks to Bill, Simon, David, Marion, and everyone else at the Clegg Agency for their expert shepherding.

And thanks, of course, to my editor, Nancy, who never says to me, "Fido, your leash is too long!"